Samantha Alexander lives in Lincolnshire with a variety of animals including her thoroughbred horse, Bunny, and her two kittens, Cedric and Bramble. Her schedule is almost as busy and exciting as her plots – she writes a number of columns for newspapers and magazines, is a teenage agony aunt for BBC Radio Leeds and in her spare time she regularly competes in dressage and showjumping.

RIDING SCHOOL

3
Steph

SAMANTHA ALEXANDER

MACMILLAN CHILDREN'S BOOKS

First published 1999 by Macmillan Children's Books
a division of Macmillan Publishers Limited
25 Eccleston Place, London SW1W 9NF
Basingstoke and Oxford

Associated companies throughout the world

ISBN 0 330 36838 9

1 3 5 7 9 8 6 4 2

A CIP catalogue record for this book is available from
the British Library.

Phototypeset by Intype London Limited
Printed and bound in Great Britain by
Mackays of Chatham plc, Kent

*Samantha Alexander and
Macmillan Children's Books would like
to thank all at Suzanne's Riding School,
especially Suzanne Marczak.*

Chapter One

Dad came out of the riding school office and gave me a quick wave before driving off. Thoughts scrambled over each other, racing around in my brain. Dad never came to the riding school, let alone to have a private meeting with the riding instructor.

Monty, my grey pony, nudged me in the back, irritated that he was no longer the centre of attention.

Monty was on loan from a girl who'd outgrown him. Dad had organized for him to be kept at the riding school free of charge in return for being used for lessons and hacks. Even though he was sort of my pony, he wasn't really – until now . . . possibly. It all seemed to fit together; the phone calls from his real owners, the questions from Dad, the talk of me having a very special birthday present . . .

I couldn't bear it any longer. Hurtling along the newly painted row of stables, I crashed into the saloon, which was an extended stable decorated in a Western theme where everybody hung out.

"Dad's buying Monty for my birthday!" I yelled, practically breaking the sound barrier, grinning from ear to ear. Then I proceeded to pirouette down one side of the saloon, did a cartwheel and finally tripped, lunged forward, and collapsed into a chair in a fit of giggles.

Kate glanced up from a horsy crossword with a blank expression. Jodie, who was cleaning a bridle, gave me a hard stare. "And exactly how do you know this?"

It was so typical of Jodie to try and burst my bubble.

"I just know." I made a sweeping gesture with my arms. "All the signs are there – it's so obvious."

Emma, who was the youngest, showed the most enthusiasm. "You're so lucky, Steph. My parents would never buy me Buzby – not in a million birthdays."

I couldn't stop a satisfied smirk. Steph Richards – Pony Owner. I would be able to do exactly what I wanted; picnic rides, jumping, horse shows – I might even try dressage. One thing was for sure – I wouldn't let any more beginners bounce around on him yanking at his mouth. The only person who was going to ride Monty was me.

Jodie carefully squeezed out her sponge and rubbed on just enough saddle soap without causing a lather. I could see she was working up to saying something. She always furrowed her brows when she was thinking.

Jodie, Emma and Kate were three members of the Six Pack. I was the fourth and Sophie and Rachel brought it up to six. We'd initially formed the Six Pack to save Brook House Riding School from being closed down. Now our mission was the continued welfare of the horses and ponies and learning as much about horses as possible. We were determined that Brook House would eventually be voted Riding School of the Year. We all helped out at weekends and holidays in return for free lessons. Guy was the riding instructor and Sandra a full-time groom.

Jodie scraped dried grass off a Pelham bit. "Don't you think you're jumping to conclusions?" she asked.

It was the last thing I wanted to hear. A sudden streak of spite shot up inside me. "Why do you always have to be so jealous? Just because there's no chance of you ever owning Minstrel, you can't bear anyone else to have anything. You've always got to be the best, Jodie Williams. If you're not top dog, you're not happy."

The words came out in a rush and Jodie's face crumpled with hurt. Kate and Emma looked stunned. A flash of remorse swamped me but it was too late now. Besides, Jodie needed taking down a peg or two.

"If you'll excuse me," I said in an acid voice, "I'm going back to my pony."

By lunchtime everybody knew.

Georgie Fenton was the third person to mention it. "I hear you're getting a pony for your birthday. Welcome to the select club of pony owners." She flung her brand new saddle onto the tack room floor, not even bothering to run up the stirrup leathers.

I grimaced with dislike. Georgie Fenton was probably the most unpopular girl at the riding school. She'd recently moved her pony, Sultan, to Brook House at full livery. The Six Pack had rallied round in an attempt to make her welcome but she soon made her feelings quite clear. She didn't want anything to do with kids who drooled over riding school ponies, and in her book, if you didn't own a pony you weren't worth knowing. She wouldn't even let the school ponies near Sultan because they were common and ugly and he might pick up bad habits.

"If you ever fancy a hack some time, let me know. And I mean a *proper* hack, not messing about doing square halts every five minutes."

I knew what Georgie's idea of a hack was – galloping flat out, non-stop, regardless of traffic and hard roads. I stared at her tall, lean figure, her blond hair shaved up the back and her dangly

4

earrings, which you weren't supposed to wear around horses. Her mouth curved into a small, fleeting smile as she waited for me to jump at the offer. She was only asking because she thought I was going to be a pony owner.

"I don't think so," I muttered and turned my back so I couldn't see her smile vanish. She didn't say anything at first, just seethed silently. I could feel her eyes boring into me.

Her voice was high-pitched when she eventually spoke. "I don't know why you have to hang around with that Six Pack lot. They're so wet, such goody-two-shoes. You don't know what you're missing out on – you could be having some real fun . . ."

"Like I said, no thanks."

"Well have it your own way," she snapped. "But I'm warning you, don't expect me to ask you again. One day you'll be begging to be my riding partner and then you'll be sorry."

"What do you get if you cross a horse with a skunk?" Emma leaned on the fence post rattling off her latest batch of horsy jokes.

I shrugged.

"Winnie the Pooh, of course."

"What horse can't you ride?"

"Milton?"

"A clothes horse."

"What's the definition of a zebra?"

"Emma, this is stupid."

"A horse crossed with venetian blinds."

I had to smile at that one.

"Gotcha!" Emma's face lit up with delight. "Now that you're actually looking human again, what's the score? Why did you bite Jodie's head off? If I was getting a pony for my birthday I'd be hugging everybody to death. I think you owe her an apology."

I sighed heavily, not knowing where to begin. How could I tell any of my friends what had been upsetting me for weeks? They weren't in the same situation. They wouldn't understand. How could they?

"Come on, tell me." Emma poked me in the ribs with her riding crop.

"Ouch, that hurt." I grabbed some grass and stuffed it down her shirt.

"Mercy, mercy!" she cried, rolling around and clutching her neck. Suddenly she sat bolt upright, obviously remembering something important. "I nearly forgot," she gasped. "Guy wants to see you in his office – as soon as poss."

This was it. This was when Guy was going to tell me that Monty was no longer needed in the riding school. He wouldn't tell me that Dad had bought him; that would be kept secret right up until my birthday. And of course I wouldn't let on that I already knew.

"Ah, Steph, good, come in and take a seat." Guy gestured towards one of the hard plastic chairs hugging the wall.

I had to catch my breath after running across the yard. I swallowed hard and sat down, clasping my hands in my lap. I waited.

Guy shuffled some papers around the desk. He seemed on edge, almost nervous. "Um, it's about your lessons . . ."

There was an awkward pause. A tiny flutter of anxiety flickered in my stomach.

"I've decided to move you down to the lower group."

It was like a bombshell. I shook my head as if I hadn't heard properly. As if I'd got water in my ears.

"You've been falling behind for a while now," Guy continued. "It's got to the stage where you're holding the others back and it's not fair to them."

I sat swaying, feeling the first wave of horror hit me. I was frozen to the seat. For over a year I'd been in the top group with Sophie and Kate and now Jodie. How could I bear the humiliation of being dropped? My head started spinning in a frantic spiral.

"You can always move back up if and when you start to improve." Guy sat down, relieved that he'd got it over and done with. "I've spoken to your dad and he agrees."

My heart sank. I was too stunned to react, to even shake my head. I knew I hadn't been trying as hard as I should, especially with the flatwork, whereas the rest of the group took it all ultra-seriously and talked passionately about turns on the forehand and serpentines. I'd been late for nearly every lesson and half the time I didn't listen. But to be put in the baby group! I'd never dreamt that Guy could be so heartless. He was making me a laughing stock.

"You know if something's bothering you, Steph, anything at all, if someone's bullying you at the stables, you must tell me." Guy leaned forward, his dark eyes flooding with comfort, inviting me to open up.

That's how much he knew. I stood up stiffly. He'd ruined my credibility and now he wanted to play agony aunt to ease his own conscience. Well, if I wasn't good enough for his precious top group then he wasn't good enough to be my instructor. I stomped out of the office resolving never to have a lesson again.

The first person I ran into was Jodie. "Look, I'm sorry," she said, catching hold of my arm and turning to face me. "I shouldn't have doubted you about getting Monty for your birthday. It wasn't

8

very nice. I think it's fantastic that you're getting your own pony."

I stared at her in despair. When she'd gone I shut my eyes and sighed. How on earth was I going to face everybody now?

Chapter Two

"It's all her fault!" I marched into my brother's bedroom and slammed the door.

James glanced up, crouched over a model aeroplane, carefully applying glue from a tiny tube. James was fourteen and behaved as if he came from another planet most of the time.

I collapsed onto the bed and started fiddling with the frills of the duvet. "That girl is ruining my life!"

James gave me a cold, hard stare. "Have you ever considered for one fraction of a second how difficult it is for her?"

I glared at him. This was not what I needed.

"I never asked for a stepsister," I threw back, feeling my mouth start to tremble. "I never asked for a complete stranger to take over our house, my bedroom, our dad. I never asked for this to happen."

"Hey, come on, it's not that bad." James moved forward, still holding the glue, and put an arm round my shoulder.

Abby Barratt had moved in with us two weeks

ago. We'd known about it for two months but that hadn't made it any easier. Abby was ten, a year younger than me, and she expected us to get on like a house on fire, even though we'd only met once, at the wedding when our dad and her mum had got married. I felt as if my life had been turned upside down; I couldn't concentrate on anything, I was totally disorientated.

"I like her," James volunteered, staring at the opposite wall.

Abby was pushy, untidy, rude and never stopped talking. I couldn't see how James could possibly like her.

"You don't have to share a bedroom with her," I pointed out. From the very first night she'd eaten packets of crisps under her bedcovers, kept the light on and asked constant questions about Monty.

"All I'm saying . . ." James began, searching for the right words, " . . . is give her a chance. She might not be as bad as you think."

The whole situation was a nightmare for me. It had taken ages for me to accept Margaret, and even after she got engaged to Dad I still refused to eat any of her cooking or hold a conversation of more than one sentence with her. Just as I was getting used to her, Abby had arrived on the scene. It was too much for anyone to bear.

"Where is she now?" asked James, flicking back his curly brown hair.

"At the garage – with Dad."

"Well just try to put yourself in her shoes. She's the one who's left her home and her brothers and friends. She must be feeling like a fish out of water."

Despite everything, I felt myself soften and reluctantly agreed to be more understanding. I could see that Abby probably didn't like the situation any more than I did.

"Here's your moment to put it into practice." James got up and walked across to the window, peeling back the net curtain.

Dad's pick-up truck had just pulled up outside. I heard the familiar engine cut out and a car door shut. Dad's husky voice was unmistakeable. And so was Abby's. Her cackling laugh drifted up and in through the open window.

They both fell through the back door, holding their sides and giggling like two hyenas. Nobody ever laughed at Dad's jokes; they were too corny. I arrived downstairs with a fixed grin on my face.

"Oh, Steph, just the person I want to see." Dad swooped a great arm round my neck and pulled me closer, then locked the other round Abby. "We've come up with a great plan." His eyes were twinkling with excitement. I expected a trip to the amusement park or something. He hugged me

12

closer and planted a kiss on top of my head. "You're going to teach Abby to ride."

"I will not," I hissed two hours later when I caught Dad alone. We were in the kitchen making hot chocolate. "It's not fair, Abby's never been to riding school, she won't know what to do. Sh-she'll hold me back."

Dad turned round, leaning against the units, his face drawn into a tight line. "It's nice to know I've got such a charitable daughter."

"You don't understand, Dad." I raised my voice, clutching at straws. "Ponies are dangerous and Abby's never been near one before – she's never even had a goldfish. She's not athletic enough. *You've* seen her – she's the ultimate couch potato." I bit my lip, knowing straight away I'd said too much. Blushing, I looked away and stared at the clock.

Dad was glowering. "How do you expect her to know how to ride a pony when she's lived in the middle of Manchester all her life?"

I felt awful. I wanted to rake the words back in, but I just stood there, sullen and still, any words of apology stuck in my throat.

"You should think yourself lucky going to riding school and having a pony on loan. Right now, you don't deserve either." I'd never seen Dad so angry; he was literally shaking.

13

Upstairs, on the landing, we saw Abby quickly disappear into my bedroom. She must have heard every word.

Dad turned back, his eyes hard and cold. "Are you satisfied now?"

Abby arrived at Brook House Riding School in a pair of my old jodhpurs and a scruffy brown jumper which she said belonged to one of her brothers and which looked as if it had never been washed.

She leapt out of the pick-up as soon as we pulled into the yard, and ran up to the first horse she saw. I cringed with embarrassment as she slapped a hand on its rump and said she'd seen them do that in cowboy films. Sandra, the groom, smiled and carefully explained how you should approach horses quietly and always from the front.

Jodie and Emma came out of Minstrel's stable just as Sophie led in two ponies from the nine-thirty ride. Their eyes immediately lit up with interest. I swallowed hard and tried not to go red as they came hurrying across.

"This is Abby," I mumbled, staring at the concrete drive. "She's staying with us at the moment."

"What's she like?" Abby tutted and stepped forward, beaming from ear to ear. "I'm Steph's stepsister," she boomed. "No doubt you've heard all about me. Steph's going to teach me to ride."

14

She said it with such pride that I felt sick inside. My mouth went dry and I tried to avoid my friends' eyes which was practically impossible. The tension between us was electric. Abby's eyes misted over with disappointment but she brushed it aside and started gabbling on about Shire horses.

"I'll show you Frank," said Sophie, linking arms with Abby and leading her off to the field where Frank was grazing with the rest of the riding school horses.

"You never told us you had a stepsister." Jodie's voice was quiet and loaded with disapproval. Emma was looking completely agog.

"It never came up . . ." I groped around for an answer. "Besides, I hardly know her and she's not horsy at all."

"Well she seems really nice," Emma remarked. "You're so lucky to have a stepsister." Emma was adopted and an only child so it was natural that she'd think any family was great. "And for someone who's not horsy, she seems incredibly keen to learn."

That was the trouble. Abby never stopped. Question after question. She wanted to be involved with everything. I gave her a guided tour of the riding school ponies, telling her about different colours and breeds and sizes.

"Rusty is a strawberry roan." I pointed to the

15

ancient 12.2 hand pony dozing under a chestnut tree. "That's the name of his colour. Can you see how the brown hairs are mingled with white?"

Abby poured all her concentration into listening to every word.

"That pony there is a Palomino. He's called Archie." I pointed to the golden pony who was rubbing his tail on a fence post. "And this is Buzby." I showed her a pretty dapple grey who was trying to kneel down to reach for a dandelion under the fence. "He's the stable rogue," I said, rubbing his head affectionately. "He's so naughty – his favourite game is forcing riders off by rubbing them against the holly bush in the arena."

Abby scoured the group of ponies, some kicking up at flies and others scratching at each other's withers.

"But where's Monty?" she burst out. "I've been here an hour and haven't seen him yet."

I was taken aback by her enthusiasm. "He's used in the riding school in the mornings," I quickly explained. "He'll be finished in quarter of an hour. If you like we can head back to the stables. I thought you might like to spend some time grooming Blossom. She's really sweet."

"But I came to ride Monty."

Her voice was direct and precise. Of all the cheek, I thought, irritation beginning to bubble and boil under the surface. He was my pony, after all. Who did she think she was?

I stomped back to the yard and made straight for Monty's stable. Maybe once she'd seen him and realized that horses were hard work, unpredictable and dangerous, she might give up on the idea of riding. We arrived just as Sandra was leading him in from the arena. His reins were hooked back under his stirrups and his head was arched. The sun, breaking through a bank of cloud, glinted on his grey coat.

Abby's face drained of colour. Her eyes were suddenly huge in her face. Her hand flew to her mouth and she drew in a sharp breath. "But he's beautiful," she murmured. "I've never seen a white horse before."

"He's a pony," I corrected. "And the right term to use is grey."

We groomed for half an hour, brushing the dried sweat from his neck and chest and setting his mane straight with the water brush. Abby was useless and continually dropped the brushes which clattered near Monty's hoofs, sending him jerking back against the lead rope.

When she was brushing his legs she let out a shriek of horror and fell back in the straw. It took me ages to get through to her that the hard, horny growths on the sides of Monty's legs were called chestnuts and perfectly normal. She was convinced he had some terrible disease.

"Are you still grooming?" Kate poked her head over the door, her eyes latching onto Abby, alert with curiosity. Kate was the oldest in the Six Pack at thirteen and tended to boss everyone around. Nothing happened without Kate knowing about it first.

"Hi, I'm Kate." She smiled confidently at Abby and ran her hand through her dark hair while scanning the scene like a radar. "Now for goodness sake, let me fetch you a riding hat. I think it's about time Steph got you up in the saddle, don't you?"

It was boiling hot. Monty was more interested in kicking up at flies trying to land on his flanks. My shirt was sticking to my back and Abby made things more difficult by constantly asking what she could do to help. I jerked up Monty's girth and groaned when he blew himself up like a beach ball.

"I'll give you a leg up." Kate marched through the thick sand of the arena acting like an instructor. Jodie and Emma had come to watch and were perched on the fence, their shirts rolled up so they both had bare midriffs.

Abby went round to the left side as Kate instructed, and bent her left leg back at the knee.

"After three," she said, chucking her up and into the saddle. I winced as Abby's right leg crashed across Monty's hip. He stood quietly, gazing into space, used to all this.

A wave of irritation swept over me. Monty was meant to be my birthday present. How could Dad let me down like this? I didn't want him to stay in the riding school. I wanted him to be mine.

I grabbed the reins, pulling them out of Abby's hands without even looking up.

"Gee up," I heard her say in a sing-song voice. When was she going to realize we weren't playing cowboys?

I walked forward, measuring each stride, keeping my head down. Abby whooped and tried to flap the loose loop of rein across Monty's neck.

"Just sit still," I snapped. "And don't do that again. You squeeze with your legs to make him go forward." Her face closed up and she sat as quiet as a mouse.

"You look good," Jodie shouted, cupping her hands round her mouth.

Kate's voice travelled better. "Keep your shoulders back and your heels down."

Abby immediately sat up ramrod straight like a guardsman. Emma and Jodie clapped enthusiastically and she gave an ecstatic grin, then leaned forward to touch my shoulder.

"Can we go any faster?" she asked.

I definitely wouldn't have let her if Emma, Jodie and Kate hadn't been watching. Clicking my tongue, I urged Monty forward, jogging alongside. Abby's face lit up with excitement. "This is fantastic!" she shouted, waving at the girls, bouncing non-stop. I did a circuit of the arena and then slowed for a breather.

"Again!" Abby beamed, her face red and her hands clasping the reins like lumps of clay. "Let's do it again."

I ignored her and continued to walk down the long side of the arena.

"Let me off the lead if you can't keep up," she said, nudging my arm. "Go on, Steph, Monty'll look after me. He's cool."

In a moment of madness I pulled Monty's head towards me and chinked off the lead rope.

"Well go on then if that's what you want. If it's so easy, do it yourself." I was hot and bothered and irritated. I let my hand drop and Monty immediately slowed his pace. I didn't expect anything to happen. I thought Monty would just grind to a halt.

But I didn't account for two things. Firstly, that Sandra would be clattering feed buckets in the shed off the stables, and secondly, that Abby would lift up both her legs and, in a determined effort, slam them down on Monty's sides.

He burst into a trot, skidding away from my outstretched arm and trundling up to the gate. He wasn't doing anything really wrong, but Abby wasn't prepared for the sudden spurt of speed. Caught unawares, she lurched to one side, lost a stirrup, grabbed some mane, but couldn't stop herself from sliding. Monty shied round a jump wing and Abby sailed over his shoulder and, with a sickening thud, crashed to the ground. She crumpled into the sand, heaving for breath, her face drained of colour and contorted with pain. Katie, Jodie and Emma were already running forward. I stood motionless, a cold, guilty sweat prickling my skin.

"What did you think you were doing?" Kate flared up, her black eyes flicking over me with a sudden contempt. "You know complete beginners don't go off the lead rein."

Jodie helped Abby to her feet. She'd got her breath back but she still looked deathly pale. Emma ran across and caught Monty who was gazing yearningly at a yellow feed bucket. I stood like a lemon, helpless and useless.

Abby's mouth crumpled and a film of tears began to form over her eyes. Then she drew herself up straight and seemed to physically shake off any hurt.

"It was my fault," she said, her voice wooden and shaky. "I asked to go by myself. Don't have a go at Steph. It was my fault – I should have known what to do."

A cold chill settled on my three friends as they

21

turned and stared at me as if I was a complete stranger. Jodie was the one to voice their feelings, talking to Abby but looking directly at me. "And how can you possibly be expected to know what to do, Abby, if somebody doesn't have the decency to tell you?"

Chapter Three

"Hey, Em, what's up with everybody?" I ran up behind her and pulled lightly on her ponytail. "Have I suddenly developed the plague or something?"

"What?" Emma swivelled round, looking uneasy. "I don't know what you mean."

"I mean there's an arctic wind blowing in my direction. Like the cold shoulder. Get my drift?" I had to laugh at the pun.

Emma smiled back but it was half-hearted and didn't show in her eyes.

"Oh, don't say you've gone peculiar as well," I complained, not really believing it.

"Everyone's just wound up over this road safety test," she said. "There's a lot to learn." She glanced towards the saloon where a knot of people were already gathered. "And if we don't get a move on we won't get a seat for the meeting."

Inside the saloon the plastic chairs had been arranged in rows and the main table pushed back against the far wall. When I'd first come to Brook House the saloon had been nothing but an empty

23

stable. Now it had a distinct Western flavour with a real lassoo coiled on the wall, a life-sized poster of Billy the Kid, and an American show bridle – which belonged to Sophie – hanging near the window. What we really needed to finish it off was a Western saddle but they cost the earth. Even so, we were pleased with what we'd achieved.

The Six Pack were sitting in the front row, Jodie at one end and Sophie at the other, scribbling notes. Almost as if she could feel my eyes on her, Abby swivelled round and stared straight at me, her mouth curving up into a smug smile. Rachel whispered something in her ear and they both dissolved into smothered giggles. Rachel took ages to get to know somebody, she was usually so shy, it wasn't like her at all. Irritation quickly became real hurt as I glanced down the rows of seats and realized nobody had left a place for me.

Sophie's dad who owned a half-share in the riding school and had agreed to take charge while Mrs Brentford, the owner, was away on holiday, stood up and addressed the twenty or so riders in front of him. "Road safety is probably the most important test you'll ever take on a pony. The test, as you know, will take place this weekend and those who pass will receive a certificate. The written test will commence at eleven o'clock on Saturday morning, so it's important you know your highway code by then." Mr Green coughed awkwardly as if he expected a reaction.

Everyone remained quiet, their eyes fixed on the person standing next to him.

"If there are no questions, I'd like to introduce you to the District Commissioner of Sutton Vale Pony Club who will be able to explain everything in more detail."

A ripple of excitement ran through the room as the woman in the smart suit stood up. The Sutton Vale Pony Club was famous for its Prince Philip Games team and one of its past members, Alex Johnson, was now a famous eventer.

The woman smiled confidently. "If everyone's ready I'd like to run through what will be expected in the practical test."

A knot of nerves twisted in my stomach. I saw Jodie and Kate draw in sharp breaths. This was our chance to prove that we were capable riders, every bit as good as the riders at Sutton Vale.

"There'll be a number of hazards, such as roadworks, noisy pedestrians, parked cars, a zebra crossing. You'll be judged on how you respond to each of these, as well as on turning left and right and trotting a short distance in traffic. You'll also be required to dismount, lead and remount. Essentially we're looking for a quiet, controlled test and a good knowledge of road craft."

Jodie stepped forward with a pile of papers,

looking very official. It was Jodie who had written to the district commissioner requesting permission to take part in their annual road safety test. She'd done nothing but preach about it for weeks as if it was her own personal crusade. We'd all got roped into entering and just about every pony in the riding school had been hired for the day.

Two and a half years ago, Jodie had been involved in a terrible road accident which had left her with a shattered left leg and very little hope of ever being able to ride again. She'd fought back with physiotherapy and was now determined to face up to her fear of traffic. As she sat down again, I could see the anxiety flickering behind the confident mask she'd fixed on her face. Kate squeezed her hand as if she could see it too. It was Jodie's determination to get things done and her ability as a rider which made us all slightly jealous.

"It's impossible," cried Emma, rushing out of the saloon as if she needed a breath of fresh air.

"Not impossible, just incredibly difficult," said Rachel as she followed her out, looking gloomy.

The District Commissioner had spent an hour explaining all the pitfalls of the test and how only twenty per cent of Sutton Vale members passed in any one year. Abby had had the cheek to ask the most questions when she wasn't even taking part.

"Well, you lot just sat there like wet lettuces," she had complained when I challenged her.

Outside, a frenzied clattering of hoofs caused the horses to run to their doors and the conversation to break off abruptly. Georgie Fenton and two of her friends came haring into the yard, their ponies foaming white with sweat and blowing heavily. Georgie tilted back her riding hat and smiled menacingly.

"Well, if it isn't the goody-two-shoes Six Pack, out to save the world."

"Give it a rest, Georgie," Sophie said sourly.

"Ooh, touchy, aren't we? What's the matter? Have you all been given L-plates to wear?" she taunted.

The girl on the chestnut pony behind her sniggered.

Sultan suddenly whirled round and tried to gallop off, his eyes popping with fear.

"Hold him," one of the girls shouted.

Georgie yanked on the left rein, carting him in a circle, his head practically touching her toe. Then she rammed her heels into his sides and drove him forward. Her two friends watched in open admiration.

"You wouldn't get much chance to ride like that on your riding school donkeys," she sneered. Sultan stood trembling, his black coat drenched and glistening like oil. Georgie's eyes glittered with enjoyment. "But I suppose you have to take a road safety test to learn how to get those nags moving."

"Oh, wake up you stupid, stupid brainless girl." Jodie cannoned forward, her eyes blazing with anger, the muscles in her neck standing out like cords. "Have you any idea about the accidents that can happen on roads and how they can wreck people's lives?" She stood rigid, outraged, shaking from head to foot.

Georgie's face registered surprise, and her mouth dropped open.

"This is what it can do to you," Jodie went on, bending down and fumbling and clawing at her jodhpurs. She peeled back the material in a frenzy, then pulled down her sock and yanked her jodhpurs up higher to expose the white flesh of her calf.

Everyone stood deathly still, frozen into silence.

The jagged, mauve-blue scar trailing the back of her leg held everybody's focus. It was hard to look away from the dented hollow as big as a fifty pence piece, or the bridge of stitch marks, still vivid. The scar had a grim fascination.

"Go on, look, feed your eyes, because that could happen to you, to anyone."

Georgie's mouth tightened but for once words had deserted her.

The Six Pack had all seen Jodie's scar before – in fact, once at a horse show, she wore shorts to prove she could face people, but usually she kept her leg covered because people invariably stared or made rude comments. I could only imagine how much courage it must have taken to show it to Georgie.

Jodie stood up looking drained. Her hands were clenched together, white with tension. "OK, that's it, the freak show's over," she said, and walked away stiffly, keeping her head down and not looking back once.

"Don't you think you ought to rub Sultan down?" Kate rounded on Georgie as soon as Jodie was out of sight, her eyes flicking over her as if she was inspecting a dead fish. "Everyone knows you're supposed to walk the last mile home. If you leave him in the stable like that he'll get a chill."

Georgie leaned forward in the saddle, resting her forearms on the pommel and smiling lazily, back to her usual self. "You just worry about that yellow hairy thing you ride with the odd legs and I'll look after my own pony, because that's the difference, you see – Sultan's mine. I can do exactly what I like."

She obviously hadn't listened to a word Jodie had said.

"You've not done under the rim," I said as I inspected Monty's feed bucket, itching to find a trace of dirt.

Abby wrinkled up her face obstinately and pulled off a rubber glove. "I'm not your slave, you know, even if you do treat me like one." Monty peeled back his top lip and nodded his head up and down as if he was laughing. "Even the horse agrees with me."

Despite myself, a flicker of humour touched my lips. "Well if you want to learn to ride, you have to be prepared to do all the jobs that go with it. It's not about just sitting there and saying 'gee up', you know – it's hard work."

"Yes, boss." Abby's eyes darkened with boredom. It was working. She was already getting tired. All I had to do was keep this up and she'd never want to set foot in a stable again.

"Now, I'll just get the grooming kit which needs scrubbing, and then there's the tack. I'll show you how to clean it properly – there's quite a skill to it." I slipped the feed bucket back into Monty's stable. It had never sparkled so much.

"Why don't you take your riding boots off and I'll scrub them as well?" Abby grunted, rubbing her knees.

"You know," I said, hiding a smirk behind my hand, "I hadn't thought of that. It's not a bad idea. Thanks, Abby."

"You're not supposed to be cleaning that," I snapped as soon as I'd stepped into the saloon and caught sight of Abby. She was leaning over the table, gently sponging the soft leather of Sophie's American show bridle, and stroking it as if it were the crown jewels.

"It looked dusty," she said, keeping her eyes fixed on the ornate silver buckles. "Besides, what else am I to do when you leave me for hours on end?"

My conscience twinged uncomfortably when I heard the hurt in her voice. Had I really left her for that long? Oh dear. Well, at least she wouldn't want to come tomorrow, I thought. It was for her own good in the long run.

"Your dad's here, Steph," said Emma as she crashed through the louvred doors. "He says he's been waiting fifteen minutes and could you please hurry up." Emma flopped into a seat, panting as if she'd just run a marathon. "I just can't wait till your birthday," she gasped. "It's going to be so incredible. I wonder if Monty will have a big bow round his neck?"

Abby glanced up casually, her eyes alert with interest.

"Come on," I snapped. "We're going."

Emma stared at me, puzzled, trying to interpret my body language as I zapped out warnings to her to shut up. The last thing I needed was Abby telling Dad that I thought Monty was my birthday present. Sooner or later I was going to have to

31

admit that I'd jumped to conclusions and I wasn't getting Monty for my birthday after all.

Even worse, it would come out that I'd been demoted to the lower riding group. Just the thought of it made me shudder. The longer I left it the better – I just couldn't face Jodie's smug expression saying, "I told you so."

"It's been lovely meeting you," said Abby, formally holding out her hand to Emma, who, caught unawares, had to wipe hers first on the front of her jeans.

"But you are coming back, aren't you?" Emma checked.

I crossed my fingers behind my back. I couldn't help it. Abby seemed to consider the question before replying.

"Oh yes, I'm coming back as soon as I can." She paused and it felt deliberate. "And the next day and the day after that and every week from then on. Steph thinks it's great that I like horses, don't you, Steph?"

I nodded numbly. She was saying this to get her own back. She didn't really mean it. She couldn't.

"See you tomorrow then," Abby said, her face deadpan. And we both walked to the car without saying a word.

Chapter Four

"When can I have a ride?" Abby nagged for the hundredth time.

Last night, instead of watching TV as usual, Abby had pored over my pony books, asking endless questions. She didn't seem to be able to get enough of horses. Dad and Margaret thought it was great and James found it funny. I thought it was a nightmare.

"Shall I go and tack him up?"

"No!" I barked, and then softened my voice. "We'll go riding after lunch; just be patient." The knuckles of my hands stretched white as I clutched onto the top of Monty's stable door. I felt closed in, trapped, almost claustrophobic.

"Why don't you find Emma and Rachel? I'm sure they're doing something more interesting than grooming," I suggested.

"But I want to brush Monty. He's our pony, isn't he?"

"OK, fine." I closed my eyes summoning up inner strength. "You do that, I'm going for a walk."

I power-marched round the field twice, trying to release the steam that was building up between my ears. This was so unfair. Nobody should be expected to play nursemaid to someone as irritating as Abby. She was taking over my life.

Ebony Jane and Frank, a retired racehorse and a part Shire, both stared at me from underneath the cool cloak of the horse chestnut tree. Frank was so tall, the lowest branches were touching his back, and he was rocking back and forth scratching his withers.

I shouldn't get so upset. This was my riding school, I'd been here the longest. I knew every horse and pony intimately. I shouldn't feel threatened by Abby. Brightening slightly, I turned and headed back to the stables. I didn't see Kate waving to grab my attention. I didn't know that within moments I would feel far, far worse than I ever imagined.

"We're having our lesson now," Kate shouted, but all I registered was her mouth opening and closing. It was as if everything was in slow motion; the weight of her words sinking in, but my reaction delayed as if holding off the moment of truth for as long as possible.

"Steph, are you all right?" Her voice faltered, and she wrinkled her eyebrows, giving me an odd look. "Come on, Guy's slipping us in before the four o'clock ride. He's going to teach us shoulder-in." She sounded as if she couldn't wait. Dressage was Kate's favourite, and Archie was really good at it. They would soon be able to enter competitions.

Sophie was already in the arena, warming up Rocket, trying to get him to bend round her inside leg. She waved. Unaware.

The raw panic which I knew was building up suddenly broke through. I could feel the heat prickling up my neck, the dryness tightening my throat. "I've got a headache," I blurted out. "That's why I went for a walk – to try and clear it."

"Well there's nothing like riding to get rid of that," Kate chivvied, trying to be so adult.

"I can't." My voice was little more than a croak. I could hardly breathe because my heart was hammering so fast. "Just leave it!" I muttered, stumbling forward, my eyes suddenly glazed with a film of tears.

I didn't see Guy until I nearly crashed into him.

"Whoa there, steady, it's not the Grand National." His angular face split into a grin as if everything was all right. As if I was still in the top group.

I wanted to cannon past him, but he propped a hand on my shoulder, anchoring me to the spot. "I've put you in Rachel's group for tomorrow morning. It'll be like a refresher course, just what you need."

Rachel had only been riding for six months.

35

They were barely cantering, let alone jumping. I could feel Kate's astonishment. The truth was out. Soon everyone at the school would know, and they'd all be sniggering behind my back. A wave of hurt seared through me.

"It's all right." I took a step away, my voice trembling. "I've decided not to have any more lessons, I'm just going to hack, it's much more fun."

Guy's eyes widened. "But what about the road safety test? What about your flatwork? You can't just throw it away."

"It's boring anyway," I lashed out. "I should have packed it in ages ago. From now on I'm going to do some proper riding."

A new sense of purpose coursed through me. I didn't need lessons. I could ride perfectly well. Before Guy had a chance to respond, I swivelled round and stalked off. He didn't see me rubbing at my eyes with my knuckles. Nobody was going to know that I'd been hurt at all.

I didn't notice Monty and Abby until I'd passed the saloon and could see clearly down the drive. Emma and Rachel were on either side, jogging to keep level, as Abby bounced up and down in the saddle, slamming her heels into Monty's sides every time he threatened to slow down.

As they turned to come back, Monty stumbled and Abby shot forward and flopped onto his neck, giggling uncontrollably as Rachel tried to lever her back into position. Emma was shouting instructions but nobody took any notice. Rachel grabbed hold of Abby's knee and they set off again, shrieking with laughter as Monty made a beeline for a tasty shrub in need of some pruning. The sun poked out from behind a blot of cloud and Sophie's American bridle glinted on Monty's head, the silver sparkling and the dark leather contrasting with his light coat. Abby let out a whoop of excitement as she nearly got towed under some low-lying branches.

"What do you think you're doing?" I hardly recognized my voice, it was so distorted with anger. I took heavy steps foward, overwhelmed with jealousy.

Abby tilted her head up, trying to see under the peak of my riding hat which was a size too big for her. I grabbed at Monty's reins just as he decided to veer off into a flower border.

"Get off!" My voice was arctic.

A hollow silence followed.

"What's got into you?" Emma cringed with embarrassment, but I didn't care.

"Get off my horse." I fired out each word like a bullet, staring at Abby until she awkwardly slithered out of the saddle.

"Now give me my hat."

Abby fiddled frantically with the chinstrap, then Rachel helped her, all fingers and thumbs.

"Don't you ever ride Monty behind my back again." I felt as if I was going to explode. It was all Abby's fault. Everything. I stared into her wide-set, brown eyes and felt real hatred. "Isn't it enough that you've taken over my dad, my home, my brother, and now you've started on my friends? Well, you're not having Monty, no way, he's my pony." I snatched at the reins, startling him from a doze.

"How can you be so mean?" Emma glared at me, disbelieving. "I always knew you had a nasty streak, Steph, but this is cruel. She's your sister for heaven's sake."

"That's a joke," I spat, not caring how much hurt I caused. "Sisters? We hardly know each other! If Dad hadn't married Margaret she'd still be in Manchester."

Abby looked up, her hair flattened, her narrow face white.

"Nobody can say I haven't tried," she whispered, suddenly seemingly so much older. "I thought you were someone to look up to. I wanted to be like you in every way." She paused, her eyes empty and resigned. "We could have been friends, but the trouble with you, Steph, is that you want to keep everything for yourself." She walked away, dignified, the only sign she was upset being the slight droop of her shoulders. Rachel went after her.

"Don't count on me as a friend after this," Emma snapped. "You're out of order, Steph, big time." She left me alone in the middle of the drive holding Monty which was what I'd wanted all along.

"It's just you and me, boy," I murmured, pressing my cheek against his nose. And as my anger slipped away, the heavy weight of guilt kicked in.

"Faster!" I urged Monty on, clattering over the loose stones, feeling the rush of speed against my face, my neck. "Go on, go on." We tore up the bridleway, thundering into a near gallop. I crouched closer to the saddle, half aware of the hedge whipping past, my eyes watering as rushing air slapped my face. It was exhilarating. It was the fastest I'd ever been.

I yanked on the reins to slow down as the narrow track petered out. Monty responded by slamming in his heels and jerking to a halt which nearly sent me sprawling up his neck. The breath dragged in my throat from the exertion, but every nerve was set alight from the thrill. Monty pulled and tugged, crabbing sideways, his eyes bursting with the same buzz.

For years, all he'd done was a rocking horse canter up that same track, dropping to trot well before the road. All the hacks I'd been on with the riding school had been slow and controlled. I must have been mad to stick it for as long as I had. I wasn't like Kate and Emma and Rachel. I didn't have to follow stuffy rules. I could do anything I wanted with Monty once the riding school had finished with him.

My lips stretched into a thin smile as I thought of Kate doing shoulder-in and Guy bossing them all around like a schoolteacher. I sucked in a mouthful of air and revelled in the jolting rhythm of Monty, straining to go faster. I was free, away from Abby's constant harping, away from her stupid questions and her trailing after me like a puppy.

"Yee hah!" I shouted up at the blue sky and pushed Monty forward, tapping my heels on his sides and feeling him respond like he never did with the others. It was as if somebody had put a match to a petrol can; he was suddenly all life, all speed, all flared nostrils and foaming mouth.

One, two, three. I counted the tiny drainage ditches as we raced down the grass verge, jumping one after the other. Monty skittered out onto the road when I lost a stirrup, and a car hooted behind me. I pulled him back onto the verge and stuck my tongue out at the woman driver. Starchy old ferret. No sense of fun.

Monty suddenly stiffened like a pointer, his

whole body electric with tension. I tightened the reins and tried to soothe him but his whole attention was fixed on the road ahead. He ran forward taking quick wooden steps and whinnied with a blast of noise that shattered the still air. A shudder of nerves rippled up my spine.

Three ponies surged round the corner, straddling the road. The riders were chatting and giggling but fell quiet when they saw Monty coming towards them. The black pony in the middle threw up its head and neighed wildly. Georgie Fenton took in the scene in front of her and then kicked him forward.

"Well, well, we've not seen you out by yourself before. Where are your precious bodyguards?" Georgie rode up alongside me, hardly able to hide her delight.

Monty was crushed between Sultan and one of the other ponies and refused to leave them. I had no choice but to turn in their direction. Georgie introduced me to the other two girls, Serena and Jane, who immediately plastered friendly smiles onto their faces.

"So you've finally seen sense and left the circles and serpentines behind," Georgie said grinning, and jabbing at Sultan when he tried to break into a trot. Monty settled down and walked out on a long rein, happy to be in horsy company. I relaxed and found myself enjoying their conversation.

"It must be really difficult for you having this new girl living with you," said Georgie, startling me with her genuine concern. "I've got a stepdad and I can't stand his kids."

I suddenly started opening up, all the bottled-up emotion spilling over as Georgie listened and seemed to understand exactly what I was trying to say. "My friends are OK, but they just see Abby's side," I went on. "In fact Emma thinks I should be over the moon about it all."

"Sad girl," Georgie tutted. "They're not giving you much support, are they?"

I felt a twinge of guilt at talking about my friends like that, but I had to agree with Georgie, they weren't even trying to see my side.

"You're getting a bit old for this club thing anyway, aren't you? I mean, it's your life, you can do what you want," she continued.

We broke into a trot, hammering forward, all in a line, Monty stretching into extension, bubbling with excitement. It felt good.

"Look, say no if you like, but I could get rid of Abby for a while. . . . Well, not get rid of her, but give you more space, stop her being your permanent shadow."

A flame of hope leapt up inside me. I was willing to try anything. I didn't think I could bear another day with Abby at the riding school.

"Leave it with me," said Georgie consolingly.

42

Serena and Jane crossed over to the verge ahead for a canter and we followed. Maybe Georgie wasn't that bad after all. At least she'd listened to my problems. And I was having fun, wasn't I? The Six Pack were getting too serious for their own good. I opened my fingers and Monty rocketed forward, grass flying up behind as he bucked and sprang after Sultan. We were both having more fun than we'd had for weeks.

As we turned homewards towards Brook House, a nagging worry started pulling at my insides. I'd stormed off leaving Abby crying in the saloon and Emma and Rachel convinced I was the most selfish person in the world. No doubt by now they'd have reported everything to the others, and then there was the humiliation of being dropped from the top group. Kate had probably figured that I wasn't getting Monty for my birthday too.

And when they saw me riding home with Georgie, well, that would really seal the rift. I doubted any of them would talk to me again. A stab of anxiety ran through me. There was nothing I could do. I couldn't just wave goodbye to Georgie and start out on another ride. And I couldn't say I didn't want to ride through the gates with them. I was trapped.

I stared down at Monty's coat covered with dried sweat. At least he wasn't hot. I gave him more rein as his head sagged down, weary.

"It's so cool being a pony owner," Georgie struck up, letting her feet loll out of the stirrups and looping the reins through one arm. "I don't know how people stand plodding around on those riding school puddings. They look half dead. I bet you can't wait till Monty is all yours."

She wittered on, swinging her legs back and forth which caused Sultan to half rear. Unlike Monty, he was still pepped up and raring to go.

"I tried having a conversation with that Emma girl the other day," she continued. "All I asked was if she went to shows, if she rode every day and who her blacksmith was, but I soon realized she couldn't answer any of them. She just stared at me blankly. So boring. And that pony she worships, the grey blob – what's his name? . . . Buzby – he looks like a cross between a dog and a camel. Should be quarantined."

I winced at the spite in her voice and wanted to stick up for Emma and Buz but the words died in my throat.

"Listen, I was wondering . . ." Georgie swung Sultan closer. "We're going to see Josh le Fleur's demonstration at Horseworld Centre the night after next. We've got a spare ticket . . ."

The Six Pack had been trying to get tickets for weeks but they were ultra-expensive and sold out anyway. Josh le Fleur was the leading trainer in the country, using new techniques in the vein of the legendary Monty Roberts. People said he could get a horse to do anything. Horseworld Centre was just down the road. It used to be a riding school but now held regular showjumping and dressage classes and different lectures and clinics every month. All we could ever do was ride past and try to catch a glimpse of the action by standing in our stirrups.

"Would you like to come? It's all paid for – you just have to turn up." Georgie's eyes bored into me, not expecting me to say no.

"No . . . I mean, yes," I said. Her comments about Emma, the Six Pack, her bad horsemanship were all wiped away like chalk off a blackboard. All I could think of was Josh le Fleur.

Georgie's eyes crinkled with amusement.

"It's the chance of a lifetime," I raved, blanking out all thoughts of my friends' reactions.

"So you're coming?" Georgie smiled triumphantly.

"Oh yes. Just try keeping me away."

Chapter Five

I was a fool if I thought Georgie was going to keep it to herself. As soon as we got back to the stables she was boasting to anyone who'd listen.

I sneaked Monty back into his stable and quickly rubbed at the sweat which was encrusted all over his chest and outlined his saddle. I didn't want Guy to see, if I could help it.

There was no sign of the Six Pack, or of Abby.

I put the saddle and bridle back in the tack room and then went to find Georgie in the feed room, as arranged. She was waiting by one of the feed bins and grabbed my arm as soon as I entered.

"Look." She pulled the lid off the furthest bin and ran her hand through some flaky white oats. I knew they were oats because they were exactly the same as the porridge Margaret had served up all winter. I stared at them as if they were an illegal drug. All I knew was that oats were energy packed and often unsafe for ponies. Monty always had a feed of pony nuts and chaff, and I explained this to Georgie.

"And that's why he's like a donkey," she scoffed.

"Now here, this is Sultan's feed bin, so help your-self. And here's a special iron supplement which will really get him going. Go and get a bucket now."

She left me alone, trailing my fingers through the oats, feeling like a conspirator. I reckoned that if I was going to take Monty on long rides he'd need more energy. And it was really good of Georgie to give me her feed.

"What are you doing?" Emma blocked the doorway, hands on hips, her face as brightly-coloured as her orange T-shirt. "Honestly, Steph, I knew you could stoop low but making friends with Georgie Fenton? You must be out of your tree."

I jumped guiltily, jerking my hand out of the feed bin. "She's not that bad," I said lamely. "She just needs someone to tell her about pony care."

"And I suppose you think you're that person." Emma grunted.

I didn't answer.

"We're having a Six Pack meeting at four o'clock in the saloon. I might as well warn you, Jodie and Kate are livid about you going to see Josh le Fleur. It's a case of if we can't all go then nobody goes. You know, that little word – loyalty. Has it dropped out of your vocabulary?"

"Oh get lost, Emma."

"And apologize to Abby." Emma stared at me,

47

making it quite clear what she thought. "She's grooming Blossom."

Irritation raged inside me. I didn't have to stand trial just because I was going somewhere with Georgie and not with the Six Pack. What had happened to free will?

I thumped down Monty's feed bucket – the one with no handle and his name painted on it – and started ladling in oats. I'd show them all what a good rider I was. And just for good measure, I added an extra scoop.

Twenty-five minutes past four. I glanced guiltily at the face of my Mickey Mouse watch. I hadn't gone to the meeting. Instead I'd sneaked off with Georgie, Serena and Jane to the coffee shop, Orchard Mall, in the new part of the village. I'd been before but the drinks there were really expensive and Sophie thought it was a rip-off. I was conscious of the tiny amount of loose change left in my pocket and tried to make my vanilla and banana milkshake last as long as possible.

Serena and Jane were talking about movies and Leonardo di Caprio. Georgie said she'd got her eye on a boy at school who was Leo's double and she was positive that he'd be asking her out as soon as term started. I tried to steer the conversation round to Josh le Fleur but Jane's eyes glazed over and she went straight back to boys.

"We'll pick you up at eight o'clock," Georgie reassured me. "Make sure you give me your address before you go."

I scribbled it down then and there on a paper napkin and tried not to notice Serena giggling and pulling faces at Georgie.

"Have Emma and Rachel ever had boyfriends?" Jane's face took on a gleeful leer as I shrugged my shoulders. Georgie burst out laughing and I tried to join in. I'd never had a boyfriend either but thankfully they didn't guess.

"Oh crikey, I've got to go." I suddenly remembered that Dad picked us up at five o'clock.

"Have a nice night in with your weird stepsister," Georgie sniggered. "And we'll see you tomorrow tacked up at twelve."

I nodded mutely and scrambled out of the shop.

Abby spent the whole night glued to the television watching soaps, and didn't utter a word, even when I accidentally tripped over her pile of books. When Dad asked if she was enjoying riding school, she nodded and added that tomorrow she was helping Emma to bath Buzby. It was news to me. I was amazed she was even going back.

To hide a burst of annoyance I went upstairs to root out my best pair of jodhpurs and riding gloves for tomorrow's ride. The Six Pack only ever wore jeans or scruffy jods, discoloured from too many washes, but Georgie, Serena and Jane all had the latest fashions. Jane must have money on tap to afford suede jods and proper riding shirts. I spent the rest of the night reading one of James's *Top Hits* magazines, trying to catch up on the latest movies so at least I would have something to talk about tomorrow.

The next day Sophie got out of her dad's car and for the first time ever didn't shout hello. Usually we'd have walked up to the stables together.

Abby and I arrived late because Margaret had some shopping to do first and it was nearly twelve o'clock by the time I slipped into Monty's stable. I noticed the difference immediately. He was tense and drawn round the flanks, ready to flinch at the slightest movement. His eyes, usually so placid, were alert and shining. As soon as I opened the door he crushed against me, trying to get out.

"Whoa boy, steady." I held out some mints in the palm of my hand and tried to push his shoulder back. He snatched at them briefly and scattered them on the floor. Georgie was already leading out Sultan whose hoofs clattered and skidded on a grate. Wasting no time, I did up my riding hat and unleashed the reins which were caught up in Monty's throat lash then pinned under the stirrups. He would have already done an hour's work in the riding school. Serena and Jane appeared in the yard next to Georgie.

"And to dry off the tail, you do this." Emma, who had Buzby tied up outside, suddenly grabbed hold of his tail and spun it round so a shower of water sprayed up all over Georgie.

"Watch out, you imbecile, you're not supposed to do that all over people." Georgie flicked water off the arm of her shirt while Abby and Emma doubled up in a fit of giggles. Buzby then decided to join in the fun and gave a huge doggy shake, cascading water all over Jane.

"That pony is the limit," she screeched. "Can't you control it, just for once? It shouldn't be allowed near people."

By the time we set off on our ride I was the only one completely dry and Jane was on the verge of tears because the suede on her jodhpurs might be stained permanently from the soapsuds.

Monty jigged along, snatching at the bit, skewing his head to one side when I wouldn't let him go forward.

"The oats have pepped him up," said Georgie, glancing over her shoulder and smiling triumphantly.

I had to use all my energy to keep him under control. My arms were already aching.

"Now you can really do some riding," Georgie shouted, resting one hand on Sultan's rump.

I didn't answer because I was terrified that if I took my eyes off Monty, his head would disappear between his knees and he'd buck until I came off.

All four ponies thundered down the narrow lane then veered sharply to the right, down the side of a hedge.

"But this is a footpath," I shouted to Serena who was directly ahead and doing nothing to stop her pony from dancing sideways into the farmer's field.

"So what? It's a fantastic gallop," she yelled back. "We've not been caught yet." She let her reins drop and immediately her pony blasted forward.

The sheer surge of speed made me gasp. Monty panicked into a faster gallop, terrified of being left behind.

We hurtled along, soil flying up in a dusty curtain. All I could hear was pounding hoofs on hollow ground. I crouched forward as tight as a jockey, urging Monty on. I didn't think what would happen if he stumbled, if he put a hoof in a rabbit hole; I was completely absorbed in the electric buzz of speed. I closed my eyes, feeling the whip of the wind on my cheeks and in my hair. Nothing in the world felt like this – we were free from everything.

Monty saw the old woman first and threw himself nearer the hedge, reeling off balance to avoid knocking her down. Sharp, stinging brambles smacked at my face and I lost a stirrup.

The woman stood transfixed, trembling from head to foot, clutching a tiny dog who was yapping in protest. I pulled on Monty's reins but he had no intention of stopping. The other ponies were careering on ahead.

"I'm really sorry," I yelled back, but the words were smothered as Monty leapt forward, seizing the bit in his mouth and thundering on. The old lady became just a blur, a dot in the distance, still rooted to the spot and staring after the ponies, probably in shock.

"Did you see that old lady?" I shouted to Georgie who finally pulled up on Sultan. Monty crashed into Serena's chestnut, his sides heaving for breath and his mouth flecked with white foam. For a few moments it was clashing stirrups and yanking reins as we tried to sort ourselves out. Sultan kicked out peevishly as he plunged into the other pony's sides.

"That old lady," I repeated, still in shock myself, "we nearly knocked her down. We must go back and see if she's all right."

Serena and Jane stared at me in amazement. "Are you serious?" said Jane.

"She could have been killed," I croaked. "Or even her dog. We should never have gone on a footpath."

Georgie angled Sultan closer and Monty shuffled back warily.

"Look, if you want to play good Samaritan, go back and find her, but she's nothing but a nuisance. She's always on this footpath and she should know what to expect. It wouldn't hurt her to get out of the way."

"But she's an old woman," I protested, hardly believing their attitude. All three of them glared at me, forming a wall of animosity. I didn't dare say that we were in the wrong. That bridleways were for horses, not footpaths, and it was in the road safety test that you should always walk past pedestrians. There was no way Monty would leave the others, so I rode on behind them, wanting to be back at the riding school, in the saloon, even talking about turns on the forehand and shoulder-in.

After a few moments Georgie slipped alongside me, and gave me a megawatt smile, as if the whole episode was forgotten.

"I'd wear a skirt tonight," she said beaming, "and jazz up your hair a bit. Don't look as if you've just come out of the stable."

Thoughts of seeing Josh le Fleur took over from thoughts of the old lady. I was filled with a warm, fizzy anticipation. It was going to be ace.

"But it'll be in the indoor school," I said, grasping what Georgie was saying. "There's no need to get dressed up – we'll need coats."

"Just do it, OK?" she snarled. "It says so on the

54

tickets." She smiled sweetly and started to praise Monty.

He was still pulling my arms out as we rode into the stable yard, and broke into a ragged trot as he spotted Rocket and Archie by the field gate. Sandra came across, almost as if she'd been waiting especially to see me. I knew Sandra would usually be busy bedding down and a cold shiver of anxiety rippled through me. There was no sign of any of my friends. Or of Abby.

Sandra rested a hand on Monty's reins, her eyes going to the crusted foam and grass on the bit. "Guy asked me to watch out for you," she mumbled, pushing her blond hair behind her ears. "He'd like a word urgently. In the office. I'll take Monty and untack him."

I gulped nervously and swung out of the saddle. My legs buckled on the concrete. I'd never ached in so many places. Monty butted my stomach and snorted loudly. Maybe it wasn't anything bad. Maybe he'd reconsidered and decided to put me back in the top group.

I knocked lightly on the office door and stepped in, twisting my hands together nervously as Guy looked up with a stern face.

"Ah, Steph, there you are. There's something I need to discuss with you."

I stood awkwardly at the other side of the desk which was cluttered high with papers, a bottle of horse shampoo and a hoof pick balanced on top. I gritted my teeth and waited.

"It's about Abby."

I started in surprise.

"To cut a long story short, Sophie's American show bridle went missing this lunchtime, and . . . well . . . it was found in Abby's bag."

I flinched.

"Abby swore she didn't take it and to be quite honest I believe her. What I really want to find out is how it ended up in her bag."

My thoughts tumbled over each other. Abby loved that bridle and she'd been the last to use it on Monty.

"I know there's been a lot of bad feeling between the two of you," Guy went on. "It would be understandable if you wanted her to stop coming here, wanted that badly enough . . ."

"I didn't do it." I couldn't believe what he was suggesting.

"OK." Guy swung his hands behind his head. He looked relieved. "Just so you know, she's gone home with your dad. She was quite upset."

A gnawing sense of guilt twisted my stomach. I'd been so awful to her. I didn't like her but I didn't think she was a thief.

"One more thing."

I was making for the door, desperate to get away.

"Monty bucked somebody off this morning. He was like a different pony. Have you any idea what's got into him?"

I shrugged in reply, then stumbled out of the office, gulping in air, feeling quite sick. If only I hadn't given Monty those extra oats.

"Hey, Steph!"

I glanced up. Georgie was climbing into her dad's car. She grinned impishly through the window in the back seat and stuck up her thumb. There was something in her face, in her eyes. Surely not. No. It couldn't have been. What had she said? *I could sort out Abby. Leave it to me.* I stared at her departing figure waving from the back window. No, I told myself sternly. Even Georgie wasn't capable of being that cruel.

Chapter Six

Blast. That's all I needed. The zip of my only decent skirt well and truly snarled up with my new top. I performed an angry jig around the bed as if that would help then swivelled the skirt round for a better look and groaned out loud. It was hopeless. The whole outfit would have to come off.

Somehow time had run away with me. Georgie would be knocking on the door any minute. Jeans would have to do.

If only Dad hadn't spent so long interrogating me about Abby and the missing bridle. My blood chilled when I remembered his words about Monty. *If he gets dropped from the riding school, I'm sorry, Steph, but there's no way I can foot the bills for shoes, hay, feed and all the rest of it. He'll have to go back to his loan owners.*

I sat down on the bed, watching the colour drain from my face in the mirror. At the beginning of the week I'd been so cocky about owning a pony. Now I was fighting just to keep one on loan. I had to get those oats out of his system, and fast.

The horn tooted outside. I drew in long, slow

breaths. It was time to go. Moving quickly now, I stuffed two five pound notes into my jeans pocket and flew down the stairs.

"Have a nice time," said Margaret appearing in the hallway, tight-lipped because I wasn't taking Abby. The door clicked shut behind me.

"What took you so long?" Georgie leaned over towards the back seat, watching me squeeze in next to Serena. She darted her eyes over my jeans like a hawk. "I thought I said to wear something decent."

I noticed with horror that all three of them were dressed up to the nines, plastered in make-up and wearing platform high heels. I squirmed uncomfortably. Georgie introduced me to her brother who was driving and didn't speak. His hair was scraped back into a lank ponytail and he just sat hunched over the wheel, scowling.

Georgie smiled graciously and said we were going on a picnic ride tomorrow and I was in charge of sandwiches.

"Sounds great," I mumbled, wondering why I felt so heavy-hearted.

"Oh and I fed Monty while you were talking to that Guy Marshall. He devoured the lot. He really loves his oats, doesn't he?"

"Yeah," I croaked, feeling my stomach clamp into tight knots of hopelessness. "I think we're going in the wrong direction." I was starting to get nervous after sailing through another set of traffic lights I didn't recognize.

The atmosphere was suddenly heavy. Something was wrong somewhere. Nobody had so much as mentioned Josh le Fleur.

"I wonder if he'll use a round pen and work them loose?" I volunteered, feeling the air turn ice-cold. Serena nudged Jane and Jane eyeballed Georgie.

."Actually, we couldn't get the tickets. They'd double-booked." Georgie kept her eyes focused on the dashboard.

My brain was whirring as I uttered the next sentence. "So where are we actually going?"

It was a few moments before Georgie spoke. "A party. Some friends of my brother's," she mumbled. "They've hired a youth club." She stared straight ahead but I saw the sly smile flicker on her face through the rear view mirror.

So that was it. There never were any tickets for Josh le Fleur. It was all a set up. Georgie just wanted to get me away from the Six Pack, to break us all up. I'd fallen for it hook, line and sinker.

Suddenly I felt claustrophobic. I just wanted to go back home. I didn't want to be in the middle of nowhere, heading for a youth club. Dad would go absolutely berserk – he'd ground me for years.

"I want to go back," I said, pulling my seat belt away from my body, panic rising.

"Don't be so silly," Georgie snapped. "You'll enjoy it. Besides, we're already here."

The car juddered to a halt outside a grey building with an old sign saying Community Youth Club. A thickset man with a moustache was taking invitations from a group of girls, all wearing very short skirts.

"Look, there's Toby." Georgie's brother suddenly came to life, switching off the engine and pushing the door open with his foot. "Hey, Tobe, over here." Swarms of people appeared round the corner, forming a queue at the entrance.

"Come on." Georgie grabbed my arm and literally hauled me out of the car. "This is going to be the party of the century."

I stood shaking, feeling sick with disappointment I didn't want this. I didn't want any of it. I'd been such a fool, so gullible.

"Sorry, no jeans I'm afraid," said the organizer as I walked through the door.

"What?" I stared at him, motionless.

"Sorry, but rules are rules. It does say on the invitations." He was already taking invitations from other people.

Georgie and Serena glanced back to see what had happened.

"I can't get in!" Panic dragged at my voice.

Georgie shrugged but didn't make any effort to

move. "I did warn you," shouted Georgie above the noise. "There's a bus stop down the road."

"But you can't . . ." The knot of people in front crushed forwards and the three girls disappeared into the crowd.

I was left alone on the pavement, hugging my arms. I didn't have a clue where I was. Cars rushed past on the main road. A sudden chill cut through my thin shirt and I realized my riding jacket was still in the car.

"Can you point me in the direction of Carlton Estate?" I asked the organizer, but he was too busy dealing with the queue of people, and ignored me. "Oh don't bother," I mumbled, and set off down the road, marching to keep myself warm.

I couldn't find the bus stop.

I turned down a side street, tight and cold with fear. I could be out here all night. Terrible thoughts kept leaping into my mind. I had to get a grip. I couldn't buckle now. Angrily, I brushed away hot tears from my cheeks and trudged on. I could always ring for a taxi. I had some money. But Mum had always told me never to get in a taxi alone. Ninety-three, ninety-four, ninety-five. I counted my strides and concentrated on avoiding the cracks in the pavement – anything to stop panic breaking out.

I walked faster. The narrow streets gave way to tree-lined avenues. Then I saw a park on my left.

I would find a phone box and call Dad. As soon as I'd decided, I felt better, warmer. I looked up and down the road so he'd know where to come. Coronation Parade.

I pulled up short, my heart starting to beat faster. Surely it couldn't be. I ran forward, dashing round the next right-hand bend. There was Sophie's house, standing back from the road with a huge willow tree in the garden. I wasn't lost at all. I knew exactly where I was. I flew up the drive, and rapped the familiar brass knocker in the shape of a lion's head.

"Come on, come on," I said to myself, hopping from one foot to the other, determined to tell Sophie everything. To admit I'd been a stupid, foolish idiot.

"Hello." Natalie answered the door. Sophie's older sister.

"Is Sophie in?"

Natalie arched her perfectly shaped eyebrows. "She's gone to Jodie's. I thought you'd have been there. Didn't you know, they're having one of their meetings? I heard Sophie talking to your stepsister on the phone." Natalie's mouth carried on moving but I'd ceased hearing. They were having a Six Pack meeting without me. They were going to chuck me out. It was so obvious. They were going to ask Abby to take my place.

"Are you all right?" Natalie peered into my face.

"It's too late," I mumbled, feeling tears trickle down my cheeks. "They won't forgive me now. They won't even talk to me."

"I think you'd better come inside." Natalie grabbed my arm and pulled me into the hallway. "You can start by telling me exactly how you got here."

"Were you OK?" Georgie's voice crackled down the phone. "Sorry we had to leave you, but we didn't have a choice."

Oh yeah, I thought savagely, gripping the phone harder.

"We're riding at eleven o'clock. Make sure you bring marmite sandwiches, cheese and pickle, and ham if you've got any."

"The cheek," I mumbled under my breath.

"What was that?"

"I'll see you at eleven," I said firmly and replaced the receiver. What was the point of falling out with her? Then I'd have no friends at all. I couldn't bear the thought of spending endless days at the riding school and having no one to hang out with.

Abby hadn't said a word since breakfast. She was already home by the time Natalie dropped me off in her Fiesta last night. Natalie had promised not to say a word to Sophie. I was still rigid with disbelief that they'd all gone behind my back.

I sat down heavily on the stairs and remembered

what Georgie had said about feeding Monty more oats. He'd been hard enough to ride yesterday and today he was only booked in for one hour in the riding school. For the first time since I'd started learning to ride, I felt a real prickle of fear.

"He snores his head off," said Emma, smiling at the young visitor who couldn't have been more than six. "And he dreams – sometimes his legs move as if he's running a marathon. I have to go in and wake him up." Buzby stuck his huge grey head over the door and yawned at the little girl, giving a full display of his molars.

"He's like a crocodile," she gulped, stepping back.

I walked forward, towards Monty's stable, not knowing whether to say hello to Emma or to keep my head down and pretend I hadn't seen her. For one awful moment our eyes clashed and we both looked away sheepishly. It was as if there was a huge wall between us. I scurried into Monty's stable and bolted the door behind me.

Immediately he crushed against me, his chest pushing into my hip. "Monty!" I pushed him away and he turned and clattered round the box, skidding on the concrete floor which had the bed piled in one corner so the floor could dry out. His blue-black eyes looked as if they were popping out of his head.

"Monty!" My voice froze to a whisper as I advanced with the lead rope. He ducked to one side and crashed towards the door, thudding against the solid wood. Somehow I had to get a bridle on him.

"Are you ready in there?" Georgie's steely voice cut across the yard.

"Nearly," I croaked, taking deep breaths. "Perhaps you could give me a hand."

After threats of rain, a pale sun pushed its way out and the whole hillside lit up in a warm ray of light. I pushed my sleeves up and tilted my chin so I could feel the heat on my face. Even the ponies settled, stretching out their necks so we could relax the reins. I found that if I kept Monty tucked directly behind Sultan he stayed at a sensible pace and didn't pull my arms out.

We'd stopped for a picnic and taken it in turns to hold the ponies. Serena brought a special horsy rucksack which she'd won in a pony magazine and which carried all the food.

"This is so cool." Jane gazed down the hill where sheep were tugging at the croppped grass and rabbits scuttled between covers of bracken and gorse. I sighed deeply, drawing in the sweet country air. Monty hadn't been so bad after all. And Georgie and the others had been falling over themselves to make up for last night. Maybe the ticket

66

mix-up had been genuine. Maybe they hadn't lied at all.

Georgie pushed Sultan on down the gritty track and we all followed. Ahead was the road that led to the riding school. We'd been out for two hours, cutting across the golf course and along a bridleway which Georgie had found on a local map. Down below, the road looked toy-sized. A lorry tooted, trying to get past a caravan, and I shuddered, grateful that Monty was good in traffic.

Further along, heading towards the disused railway line, was the two o'clock ride, obviously going home. Sandra was out in front on Frank who was easily recognizable because of his size. Seven, no, eight ponies followed, all in a neat line. I could pick out Buzby, Archie and Rocket. I didn't want to bump into them. My hands instinctively tightened on the reins, shortening Monty's steps.

"Last one down is boring," Georgie whooped, and holding one hand in the air like a rodeo rider, she urged Sultan on down the steep track. Serena followed at a thundering canter and Monty threw up his head. I swallowed back a wave of nerves and closed my legs round his sides.

Very soon we were all going at a breakneck gallop. I clung onto a fistful of mane as Monty plunged downwards, helter-skeltering over the rough stones. Sultan skidded to a halt in front of a five-bar gate and whirled round, his eyes rolling in a frenzy. Georgie leapt off and started tugging at the chain which held the two posts together.

"I think Jake's got a stone in his hoof." Serena dismounted and gingerly picked up his leg.

"It's hardly surprising," I gasped, feeling as if every joint in my body had been jolted out of its socket.

Georgie's features blackened. "He's fine, Serena, stop fussing." She swung back onto Sultan and grabbed at the reins. "And leave the gate. Nobody knows we've been here."

"You can't do that," I exclaimed, already noticing the sheep inching closer.

Sultan spun round and dived through the open gateway, doing half leaps on his hind legs. Georgie laughed, enjoying every minute. I stared down at my hands, hating myself for being there, for not telling Georgie what I really thought of her bad riding. For not having the strength to have no friends instead of the wrong friends. Why was I such a fool?

Monty followed the others, ripping the reins effortlessly through my raw fingers. I didn't have any energy left to control him. Tears of frustration burned in my eyes.

"Come on." Georgie's harsh voice grated. "I want to get back to the stables to see if your sweet little stepsister's copped it."

"What do you mean?" Something deep inside

me knew exactly what she meant. "Abby didn't take that bridle. She's not a thief."

"Ooh, so protective all of a sudden." Georgie swung round, her eyes glistening dangerously, annoyance flaring up. "I thought you'd have been thanking me. It was what you wanted. Only you didn't have the guts to do it yourself."

I slumped forward, sickened. If only I'd given Abby a chance. If only I hadn't been so stupidly possessive of Monty. Now I'd ruined any hope of us ever being friends.

Monty suddenly sensed my lack of concentration. In a lightning movement he sank his weight back on his quarters and reared up. I lost a stirrup and floundered desperately, trying to catch hold of the reins.

"Watch out!" Serena's face quivered with fear as Monty stepped back towards a ditch.

"Monty!" I screeched, paralysed with terror. The black hollow behind seemed to be rising up to meet us. Not a moment too soon he swung down onto all fours, blowing and snorting. We could have been upside down. Seriously injured. And all Georgie could think of was galloping on down the stony track.

"Wait!" I was still grappling to find my stirrup. Sultan took off in a blaze of speed. Monty fretted and yanked at the reins, crabbing sideways. It was hopeless. Soon all four ponies were careering down the track. Hard hoofs pelted along the ground, chippings flying up in all directions. My breath locked in my throat. I was totally out of control.

"Georgie! Monty!" Words screamed in my head. I leaned back and hauled at Monty's foam-spattered mouth but his neck was fixed hard and rigid. I saw the others easing back to a canter but Monty thundered on, relentless. We were approaching the road. I blinked back tears and started battering my fist against his shoulder – anything to get a response.

It didn't work. "Help!" I found my voice just as Serena and Jane turned round in their saddles to see why I wasn't slowing down. My lungs burned as if on fire.

Monty cannoned through the other ponies, not even faltering. Then I realized why. Out of the corner of my eye I could see the riding school ponies bunched together on the verge, watching my mad dash towards the road. Monty was racing to join his friends. If I could just turn him into the hedge before he reached the road. I was already looking to each side to see if any traffic was coming. The end of the track loomed close.

In a split second Monty shied violently to the left. I didn't expect it. I collapsed forward, flopping over his neck and felt gravity pulling me down-wards. I hit the ground with stunning force, shoulder first, and felt the pain rush up my neck.

Monty galloped on, straight into the road, in a blur of flying stirrups and hoofs. He skidded as soon as he hit the tarmac. His hind legs collapsed beneath him and he crashed heavily onto his side.

"Monty!" I was running now, gripped in a vice of panic which I'd never known before.

He didn't get up. His neck swung upwards and he grunted, his eyes glazed. He was winded.

"No!"

The grinding hum of a vehicle broke through my terror. To the left I saw the riding school ponies gathered together in a ragged clump, their riders staring in disbelief. And to the right . . . Oh no. My blood froze. There was a lorry, hurtling along in top gear. And Monty was still in the middle of the road.

Chapter Seven

The screeching of brakes went on and on.

I ran into the road, waving my hands, watching the huge cab draw closer. The wheels locked and grabbed at the road surface, but it was still going too fast. There wasn't enough time.

"Stop!" I yelled, "Just stop!"

Someone ran into the road. I saw a bike abandoned on the verge, wheels spinning. And there was Abby. She went straight to Monty's head and pulled at the reins, coaxing him up.

That's what I should have done.

"Come on, boy. Up you get. Quick now." Her voice was as cool as a cucumber and her whole concentration was focused on Monty. The wild terror in his eyes abated. Gingerly he placed one fore leg in front of the other and heaved himself up.

"Quick!" I shouted, shuddering with fear. The lorry looked as if it was about to jackknife. I could see the driver's face, strained and white, as he gripped the wheel. The noise of the squealing engine was deafening.

A moment later, the lorry sailed past the spot where Monty had fallen. It skidded and spat and ground to a halt a hundred metres or so further up the road. The driver levered himself out of the cab on shaky legs, amazed that nobody had been hurt.

Abby was still holding Monty, talking nonsense to him, stroking his sweat-stained coat with a rhythmical motion. A silence fell over everybody. It was a combination of relief and shock. I reached for Monty and buried my head in his warm, sticky coat, closing my eyes to the nightmare that had just happened. Abby stood next to me, breathing steadily. Monty owed his life to her courage and clear thinking.

"I don't know how I can ever thank you," I mumbled, starting to tremble.

"Don't." She shrugged her shoulders. "I did it for Monty."

"What did you think you were doing?" said an angry voice. I jerked my head up, staggered to see Mr Green in his Jaguar, his head out of the window, his dark eyes blazing. He must have seen everything. I swallowed down a new wave of horror, but just ended up shaking.

"Is this what you get up to behind our backs?" Mr Green leapt out of the car, about to slam the door, but changed his mind when Monty shied away. A muscle twitched violently under his left eye and his hands were clenched white with tension.

"Is this what Brook House teaches people? To ride like maniacs? To be a danger to the public?" I wanted to crawl into a hole. I couldn't cope with much more. I hated myself enough already.

"Dad, I can explain." Sophie was trotting Rocket down the road, her face awash with anxiety. "Are you all right?" She scanned my dishevelled appearance, ripped jods and blood-spattered shirtsleeve. "Dad, she's just had a bad accident. This is no time—"

"Don't tell me what's right and wrong." He was literally hopping from one foot to another, colour scorching up his neck.

The lorry driver, seeing someone acting with authority, came striding up. "I want the name of your insurance company. If there's any damage to my truck . . ."

Sophie jumped off Rocket and wrapped an arm round my shoulder. The sudden kindness was too much and I burst into tears.

"How did it happen?" asked Sandra as she rode up on Frank with the rest of the ride behind her. Frank's big Shire nose nudged the lorry driver in the ribs which half scared him to death. Traffic held up by the disturbance started tooting, which set all the ponies barging into each other. I glanced round for Georgie but she'd disappeared. There was no sign of Serena or Jane either.

"Here." The lorry driver passed me a hanky with an oil stain in one corner. "I can't stand seeing people cry. Are you all right?"

Mr Green ran his hand down all four of Monty's legs, checking for damage, then turned to me. "I'll take you back in the car. Did you hit your head? Are you hurt?"

"No, no," I yelped. "I can ride, honestly." The thought of sitting next to Mr Green and his boiling wrath made me shrink inside.

"This pony is no use to a riding school. I've no choice but to let him go. He's dangerous."

"But you can't," I pleaded, desperation crashing through me. "He's not usually like this. You don't understand."

"You've got to give him another chance." Abby wrapped her arms protectively round Monty's neck.

"Dad, don't be so awful. You can't make a decision like that without consulting Mrs Brentford."

"I'm running a business, not a charity, and in Mrs Brentford's absence I have full authority here." Mr Green's face tightened with resolve.

"Even so, it does seem a bit severe." The lorry driver was softening and even reached out to stroke Monty who had recovered and was tearing at some cow parsley.

"What's it got to do with you?" Mr Green glared at him. He pushed his grey-black hair off his forehead and squared his shoulders. "OK, prove to me he's safe. Let me see him pass the road safety test. And not with an experienced rider. I want a complete beginner on board. Someone like this girl. What's your name?"

"Abby."

"Can you ride?"

"No."

"Well, here's your lucky chance. You've got four days to learn."

"Dad!" cried Sophie.

"It's my final offer. Now, if you'll excuse me, I'm going back to the office." Mr Green manoeuvred his car round the lorry and a backlog of vehicles flowed past, all carrying angry drivers, one even shouting abuse.

I turned back to Monty feeling drained. For a moment Abby's eyes clashed with mine. The bitterness and hurt were undeniable. There might as well have been a hundred miles between us.

"So it's all right for me to ride him now you need me?" Abby crossed her arms defiantly, hugging her chest.

We were in the saloon, trying to absorb the

76

bombshell. Sophie had called a Six Pack meeting as soon as we got back to the stables which really surprised me. Jodie, Kate, Rachel and Emma had listened to the story in silent amazement. I had had to confess everything – even feeding oats to Monty.

"I could try to get Dad to change his mind but there's not much hope." Sophie pressed a finger to her forehead and closed her eyes. "You're totally sure your Dad's not buying Monty?"

I nodded briskly, not daring to speak. It was going to be the worst birthday ever.

"At least she won't have to learn to canter." Rachel piped up. "That'll cut the work down a bit."

"I haven't said I'm doing it yet," Abbey answered obstinately.

"I can't say I blame you." My voice quivered with hopelessness. My shoulder ached and I wanted to crawl into a hole.

Emma started to read out Leo from the horoscope page of *In the Saddle*. "There's a horsy challenge in your life which you need to face up to. Take the plunge and it'll all work out OK. That fits you too, Abby. You're Leo as well, aren't you? No wonder you don't get on – you're both too alike." Emma went quiet when she realized she'd said too much. Abby looked furious.

"I can't believe you were so stupid," Jodie burst

out suddenly, unable to hide her feelings. "You've seen what happened to me in a road accident. Doesn't that mean anything?"

Jodie had fallen in with a bad crowd at her old riding school. It had seemed fun at the time to try and ride along the white line in the middle of the road. Now she had a metal plate in her leg.

"I didn't think I had any friends left," I croaked, my teeth chattering. "You were going to give my place in the Six Pack to Abby, p-probably still are. You all met up last night without me."

"You were going to see Josh le Fleur!" Jodie retaliated. "Or had you conveniently forgotten?"

"Stop it!" Sophie raised her voice. "There's been enough falling out. And Steph, if you must know, we called a meeting last night to discuss you and Georgie. How we could get you to see sense. Because we were worried about you."

A stony silence followed.

"I-I never realized," I said, feeling ashamed. Hot tears ran down my cheeks. The last ounce of strength drained out of me and I sat down in a battered old armchair and sobbed uncontrollably. Rachel and Emma immediately came across and wrapped an arm each round my shoulders. Kate thrust a tissue in my face.

"Whether you like it or not, the Six Pack stick together." Sophie pulled a mock stern face. We're friends for life through thick and thin, remember?

That's the pledge we all made to each other. Now, just because you temporarily messed up, doesn't mean you're not one of us any more." She held out her hand for our special handshake and we all placed our hands on top, palms downwards.

"Six Pack for ever," everyone yelled.

"Where's my riding hat?" Abby asked, standing with her hands on her hips and a piece of hay in her mouth. "If I've got to become a Harvey Smith in four days we'd better get on with it, don't you reckon?"

Monty danced and skittered sideways as Kate led him into the arena and Abby followed, turning pale at the sight of him. "What have you done to him? Put rockets in his hoofs?"

"He'll calm down in a day or two," I reassured her. "Just as soon as the oats get out of his system."

Jodie suggested we lunge him before Abby mounted and I raced back to the stables for the lunge cavesson and long whip. Lunging is when a horse goes round in a circle on a long line, held by someone standing in the middle. It's really good for making horses more obedient and supple, but if you aren't careful it can make you dizzy. Also, it's dangerous if you get the lunge rein caught up in the horse's legs. Jodie was the only one who could do it properly.

Maybe, just maybe, this crazy plan would work.

I flew into the tack room, at least feeling that we were doing something positive. I wasn't prepared for running slap bang into Georgie.

"Well, look who it isn't," she leered, her face immediately lighting up. "It didn't take you long to go running back to your old crowd. What was the matter? The pace too hot with us? Couldn't you keep up?" She glanced back towards Serena, looking for support, but Serena kept her head down and fiddled with the velcro straps on a pair of brushing boots.

I stepped back. Just the sight of Georgie made me remember my recklessness, my stupidity, and the glaring horror of seeing that lorry hurtle towards Monty. And she didn't care. She hadn't even apologized.

"I'm back with the Six Pack because they're my real friends," I burst out, surprising myself with a sudden surge of strength. "You only wanted to hang out with me to get up their noses, to break us all up."

Georgie smiled drily, confirming everything I'd just said. "And it worked, didn't it? You were sucked in. You, who said you never would be." Her eyes glowed with triumph as if she'd achieved some special feat.

"More fool me," I mumbled, despising myself. Only this time Georgie couldn't get to me. I had her measure. I knew what she was about. I turned back, not in the least bit riled. "The sad thing about you, Georgie," I answered, keeping my voice low and feeling almost sorry for her, "is that you'll go through life and you'll never really know what true friendship is."

"Legs, legs, more left rein," Jodie shouted. Abby was so busy concentrating on her hand position that she didn't realize she was tipping to one side.

"You're still bouncing up and down." Kate urged Monty on from behind with her riding crop. "Your hands keep shooting up round your chin." Abby grunted something, but it was swept away as Monty lunged forward, half rearing, and she bounced along like a rubber ball, clinging tightly onto the saddle.

"Try gripping with your knees," Rachel shouted, moving a jump wing out of the way.

"That's throwing her out of the saddle," Sophie argued. "Just think of yourself as a jelly, Abby. Let yourself go."

"Your heels have shot up again," Jodie commented.

"What do you think I am? A contortionist?" Abby pulled up, crimson in the face. "You're going to have to sort yourselves out, because I can't cope with six instructors. It's worse than being at school."

Of course she was absolutely right. Even Kate looked sheepish.

"Who can remember how to do rising trot?" asked Rachel as she jumped off the fence and walked across with Emma who was writing everything down as if it was a school assignment.

We all looked blank.

"I think we ought to take it in turns to lead her," said Sophie sensibly. "We're not getting anywhere like this."

"We could position ourselves like a relay race," Emma suggested. "That way no one runs out of puff."

"And when do I get a break?" Abby said drily, but nobody heard. Emma was already allocating positions around the field.

"Steph, you can be on the last run. From the chestnut tree to the gate."

The sheer task ahead of us was beginning to hit home. How could we possibly get Abby to ride properly when she barely knew the difference between walk and trot, never mind anything about sitting and rising? A cold feeling of hopelessness settled over me.

"Before we start," Abby added, pushing back her hat and accidentally dropping the reins, "I think my pedals are too long."

"Up, down, up, down, up, down." Kate dragged Monty on, trying desperately to stop him from breaking into a canter. Abby bumped along methodically, heaving herself up and then plopping down like a sack of potatoes.

Sophie took over from Kate. "Up, down, up, down, up, down." They trotted along the bottom side towards Rachel, and then onto Emma. Abby didn't look remotely like she was doing rising trot. In fact, she just seemed to be bumping more and more.

"Hold onto the front of the saddle," Emma advised between gasps. They were trotting towards me now, getting faster and faster. Emma's face was bright red.

"Here." She thrust the reins at me, bending down with her hands on her knees.

I kept at Monty's shoulder, trying not to interfere with his stride. Abby was bumping totally out of rhythm but looking straight ahead, her face rigid with concentration. I couldn't believe her determination.

Monty stumbled and she grasped hold of his mane to stay on. Abby was still fighting to win back her balance and I was just about to slow down to walk, when a parcel van rattled up the drive, close to the fence. Usually this wouldn't have caused a problem so I didn't think anything of it. But Monty's recent bad experience with traffic had obviously had a damaging effect on him. In a split second, he'd lurched back onto his quarters, eyes

83

popping out of his head. The reins scorched through my fingers as he shot up on his hind legs, fear oozing from every pore of his body.

Abby didn't stand a chance. Monty smashed his neck into her face and she was tossed backwards like a discarded doll. Instinctively, she curled up into a ball as Monty screamed in panic and went right over, slamming down hard on his right side, just centimetres away from Abby. It all happened so fast. If Monty had fallen the other way, his flailing legs would have . . . It didn't bear thinking about.

"*Abby!*" The Six Pack raced towards us, electrified with terror. Abby didn't move.

"*Abby*!" Now I was shouting. I stumbled across, trying to remember my first aid from school. Her face was white. I didn't move her. Leave that to the paramedics. But what if she was choking? What about the recovery position? I peered down, straining to see any sign of life. "Oh please, Abby, don't let anything be wrong. I'd never forgive myself. You've got to be all right. Abby?"

Her eyes flicked open and she grinned impishly. "I didn't know you cared so much, sis."

Relief made me dizzy. She propped herself up on one elbow and blood surged from her nose, which was already swelling up.

"Thank goodness!" Sophie was the first to reach

us, and squatted down, telling Abby to pinch her nose and lean forward.

"Who said you're not a proper rider until you've had your first fall?" Abby managed to splutter even though Sophie was urging her to be quiet.

Kate held up three fingers for Abby to count. I went to tend to Monty who was shaking, his head flopped down between his knees. The sweat was pouring off him. It was obvious he was still traumatized.

"We ought to get her to hospital. She might be concussed," Emma said, coming over.

"No way!" Abby struggled to get up, overhearing us. "Do that and Monty'll be on the first truck out of here."

"I'm hunky-dory anyway." Abby stumbled to her feet, still dripping blood. "Just give me two minutes and I'll be back in the saddle."

Rachel passed her another tissue. I marvelled at her courage and determination but a new depression was pushing me close to the edge. Not only did we have to teach Abby to ride, but we had to cure Monty of traffic-phobia. It was too much. Sophie stood grim-faced beside me, obviously thinking the same thoughts.

"So where do we go from here?"

Chapter Eight

"I can't move," groaned Abby, peeking out from under the bedclothes. We'd gone through this ritual for the last three mornings. I had to support her shoulder while she swung her legs out and gradually shuffled onto the floor. Then I had to help her get dressed because she couldn't lift her arms over her head.

"I've heard of being saddle-sore, but this is ridiculous," I said rooting out a sock from under the bed.

Abby was having to pretend that everything was OK in front of Margaret and Dad. James knew something was up but was too absorbed in his model aeroplanes to say anything. After endless riding Abby still hadn't mastered rising trot. We were now in a state of total despair. It was the theory test that morning and the practical the next day – my birthday. Short of a full-blown miracle there was no way Abby or Monty would pass. Abby insisted on green socks for good luck and started counting magpies out of the window.

"Why don't we throw in a black cat and a

rabbit's foot as well?" I groaned and picked up the road safety manual for the thousandth time. "On which one of the following can you ride or lead? A. A motorway. B. A footpath. C. A bridleway."

"Give me a break." Abby screwed up her face. "I'm not that thick."

"OK, OK, something less obvious. If you are riding one horse and leading another, where should the led horse be? A. On your left. B. On your right. C. Behind you."

"Oh, you can't fool me. That's a trick question. You shouldn't be leading a horse at all."

"No, Abby! The answer's on the left!"

"OK, keep your hair on. It's not the end of the world. Try another one."

"Can I just say that it *will* be the end of the world to me if you don't pass this test!"

We both collapsed on the bed wondering who we were trying to kid. We were almost pretending it was a school spelling test or something, not Monty's future hanging in the balance.

"Here, you might as well have this now." Abby passed me a grubby envelope which looked as if it had been stuck down with superglue. Inside was a thin piece of white card with a drawing on the front of Monty and me looking out over a stable door. It was a caricature done in pencil and it was absolutely brilliant.

"I'm a bit of a dab hand at drawing," she said, embarrassed. "Pity I'm not as good at riding, eh?"

I was still too stunned to speak. All the time she'd lived here I'd treated her like an idiot and acted superior, when actually she was really talented.

"It's really special," I whispered, finding my voice. "And . . . I'm really pleased you're here . . . as part of the family."

"Yeah?" Abby raised her eyebrows. "You know, if you look at that drawing long enough, we even look like each other – especially the snub nose."

"Don't push it." My face broke into a grin and I rammed her in the back with a pillow.

"Ten minutes to go!" Rachel shot back into the stable holding a carrier bag over her head to keep off the rain.

The test was being held in the saloon and Sutton Vale Pony Club members were still turning up in expensive cars with horsy-looking parents and enough knowledge to go on Mastermind.

"What's the sign to get a driver to slow down?" Kate was having a panic attack and scouring through Jodie's memory cards.

"Easy. A rider moves her right arm up and down with her palm facing the ground."

We were all convinced Sophie had a photo-graphic memory.

"What if we all fail?" Emma wasn't exactly inspiring confidence.

"With all the lucky mascots you've brought along, you won't even be able to see the test paper." Kate picked up a Kermit which had faded to yellow.

"I can't do this." Abby stood by the window looking as if she wanted to climb out and escape. Her teeth were chattering and her skin was shining with beads of perspiration. Monty wafted his head up and down as if to disagree.

"What do you mean *can't*? You'll breeze it." Kate shut up when she realized she sounded like a schoolteacher.

"Please Abb, for Monty," I said. Her eyes followed mine to where Monty was gently nibbling at a hay net, shaking off a fly without a care in the world.

"Why does it always have to be me?" she whimpered, her eyes glued to Monty's innocent, unsuspecting face. The mere thought of the gnawing sense of loss that I'd feel if Monty went back to his loan owners practically knocked the breath out of my body. I felt numb.

"If everybody's finished you can now put down your pens."

Abby's face creased into a megawatt grin as she stuck up her thumbs in triumph. "We did it! We did it! We did it!" She started hopping about on the spot as soon as we got out of the saloon. Emma joined her and various lucky mascots went shooting all over the yard.

Sophie was holding the test sheet against the answers in the manual, her knuckles rigid and white with tension. Jodie leaned over her shoulder, moving her finger down the page. "The correct answer to question one is . . ." I held my breath. We all dived forward because none of us could remember the question. A roar went up when Jodie said C.

"A, D, B, C, A, A, B, C, D, A."

A gush of relief swamped me when I saw the joy in Abby's face. We'd all passed, Jodie and Sophie with top marks.

"This is as good as winning a cross-country," said Emma. "Shouldn't we get a rosette or something?"

"That comes later," Sophie pointed out. "When we prove we can ride in traffic."

Instinctively, I glanced across to where Monty was standing, ears pricked forward, alert to something in the distance. What was going through his mind? How was he feeling? We'd given him some time off from even seeing a car after he nearly scrabbled across the bonnet of Rachel's mum's car two days ago. The truth was, none of us knew what to do. The best we could come up with was to give him time to forget the accident. To make sure no one hassled him. None of us would admit to each other that we were scared to handle Monty, that Sophie's dad was possibly right, that Monty was too dangerous to have in a riding school.

"OK. Lead him forward." Sophie stepped away from Guy's horsebox, leaving the ignition key in and the engine gently thrumming.

My fingers immediately tightened on the lead rope. "Come on, boy, walk on."

There was no response. Monty had already thrown up his head, eyes rolling. The veins in his neck stood out like cords, and fear surged through his body.

We were in the stable yard, near the barn, where there was enough room to lead Monty past the vehicle. He'd been fine when the engine was off, calmly walking past, more interested in raiding my pockets for horse nuts.

Now it was a different story. Abby caught my eye. A streak of nerves rippled up my spine. I could feel Monty arching his back, tensing, digging his heels in. "Please, Monty, please walk forward, walk on." I forced myself to take a step, bearing down on the lead rope.

"Come on, Monty, come on, baby." Kate held out her hand encouragingly. For a second I really thought he was going to go. He seemed to lower his neck and relax, trusting we weren't going to hurt him.

"That's my boy." Sophie's voice rose with hope.

Then it was all over. Nostrils wide, eyes bursting from his head, he charged backwards, the lead rope scorching my bare hands.

"Watch out!" Jodie's face was white with terror.

Monty swirled round, knocking me off balance, and then, desperate with panic, lashed out with both hind legs. The sound of broken glass filled my head. The left headlight was out.

Jodie rushed forward, grabbed Monty's bridle and dragged him away. Already his coat was streaked with sweat. His flanks were quivering and drawn in like a greyhound's. His eyes were dilated in a way I'd never seen before. Even worse, Guy and Sophie's dad were running towards us. Guy looked absolutely furious.

"Who gave you those keys?" He glared all around, his jaw fixed and his eyes narrowed to tiny slits.

Kate blanched as if she'd seen a ghost. She'd told us she'd asked Guy's permission to take the keys from the office.

"I took them," Sophie blurted out, trying to cover up.

"Don't lie, Sophie, you're so transparent." There was no fooling her dad. "That pony is dangerous.

I want you to turn him out in the bottom field and leave him there until we decide what to do."

"It's not for you to decide," I said, and immediately regretted it. His eyes were as cold as ice.

"While I'm in charge of this riding school, young lady, I'll make the decisions."

"No." Sophie drew herself up. We all knew how much she loved her dad, how she always wanted to please him, how difficult it was for her to go against his authority. "You gave us till tomorrow afternoon. After the road safety test. You can't go back on a deal."

Mr Green's heavy, dark eyebrows shot up in amazement. Guy quickly tried to diffuse the tension by examining the shattered headlight. Sophie remained resolute, meeting her dad's fierce glare. In exasperation, Mr Green mumbled under his breath, "OK, have it your way. But mark my words, it'll take an act of God to get that pony right."

Sophie threw her arms round his neck. "Thanks, Dad, thanks a million."

"Um, sorry to interrupt," said Guy, shuffling his feet anxiously, "but who exactly is going to pay for this completely wrecked headlight?"

"He's right though, it is going to take an act of God." I was plaiting Monty's mane to keep it lying on the right side just for something to do and to

93

try and stay sane. Abby was pulling bits of celery out of a salad sandwich and offering them to Rusty who was dozing in the next door stable.

"What we need is some kind of horse doctor, someone who can speak Monty's language." Abby was just rattling on, not realizing the importance of her words. Not until my mane comb went crashing to the floor and she turned and saw the grin splitting my face.

She smiled a slow smile, beginning to read my mind. We both shouted out into the charged silence at the same time: "Josh le Fleur!"

Chapter Nine

"It's crazy, it'll never work," said Rachel once she'd listened to the plan which we'd cobbled together.

Abby had already rung Horseworld Centre and discovered that Josh le Fleur was doing his last matinée performance that afternoon. But it was fully booked – not even a single cancellation.

"He has to go in and out of the indoor school, doesn't he?" Kate said. "All we have to do is hide somewhere until we see him alone, then spring out and plead for his help."

"And he's just going to come running to do our bidding, even though we have no money and he doesn't know us from Adam." Jodie wrinkled up her nose in disbelief.

"Well can you think of a better plan, Einstein?" Emma leaned forward, clearly not wanting to dwell on negative thoughts.

We were all sitting on the fence waiting for the twelve o'clock lesson to come in. We always did jump duty which entailed putting up the poles which were endlessly falling, even though the jumps were only two foot six.

Rocket was the first to come in, carrying a nervous rider called Sandra who rode every Saturday but never seemed to improve. Archie, Kate's favourite, came next, glued to Rocket's tail, doggedly refusing to turn right and setting off at a trot to the far corner where his best friend Buzby was grazing.

"She's got her reins all over the place again," Kate tutted. "How can I attempt to get Archie on the bit when he gets ridden by lemons like that?" Actually Kate was a very good rider and extremely adept at putting Archie on the bit and executing complicated dressage movements.

"Look who's coming next." I had to do a double-take to be absolutely sure. Georgie Fenton rode in on Sultan, keeping her eyes fixed on her hands and her mouth in a tight line.

"After all she's said about lessons." Sophie let her breath whistle out in amazement. We were all gobsmacked. She walked stiffly round the arena the opposite way to everyone else, hopelessly trying to stop Sultan from jogging.

"She doesn't even know how to form a ride," Emma bitched. "And look at her elbows – she could do a chicken impression with them."

I felt hot and sick at being so close to her. Since the accident, I'd purposely stayed out of her way, ducking behind feed bins if I had to, to keep out of sight.

"Sssh," Sophie put her hand over Emma's mouth as Guy walked in in a steaming mood.

"He's still angry about the headlight," Rachel whispered. "I feel sorry for this ride – he'll really put them through it." Guy was well known for working riders until they were blue in the face at the best of times. Now he asked everyone to trot, glowering like a bull when Archie stuck his head down to try and roll.

"Shorten your reins and keep your leg back," he yelled.

By the time the jumping started, the atmosphere was laden with bad feeling. Guy had already had words with two sets of parents who had tried to take over the lesson and instruct their own children. This happened every Saturday and Guy had some great put-down lines like: "This is what I'm paid to do. Will you kindly let me get on with my job?"

Rocket was a brilliant jumper and there was no excuse for his rider collapsing on his neck and then bursting into tears when she realized she hadn't fallen off.

"What a wimp," Kate tutted.

Minutes later an irate parent told Guy that she'd only just come out of plaster from her last fall and angrily accused him of being a slave driver.

Then it was Georgie's turn and all credit to her, she did quite well, although Sultan was pulling like a train. Emma and Rachel put up the jump following Guy's instructions and that's when things went wrong. Archie decided now was the time for a quick exit and scuttled straight out of the open gate and back to the stables with his rider screaming her head off.

Guy started shouting at the girl on Rocket for cantering past the other riders instead of waiting her turn. Poor little Blossom was cowering into the hedge, frightened to move.

Georgie was walking down the long side waiting for the ride to reform and before I knew it, she was there, trying to talk to me. I stiffened and my mouth dried up.

"I know you don't want anything to do with me," she started. I was holding a yellow and black pole with the paint peeling off at one end. I concentrated hard on it, trying to push all thoughts from my mind. I could sense the Six Pack behind, overprotective, wondering what was going on.

"I don't want to cause trouble, here," she began again, rooting in her jods pocket, digging down deep and standing up in her stirrups. Eventually she pulled out some tickets, limp from the heat of her body. She leaned down, imploring with her eyes for me to take them. I reached out and stuffed them awkwardly into my jeans pocket without looking at them.

"They're for the Josh le Fleur demo this afternoon. Dad got them for me, but I figured you'd appreciate them more. I'm selling Sultan, you see. That's why I'm on this lesson – to try and get him going better. I'm not interested like I used to be. It doesn't seem to be any fun any more." She ran on, tripping over her words. Somehow it was important for her to tell me this.

The Georgie Fenton spark had vanished. It was almost as if she'd been putting on an act all along and this faded, quieter version was the real her. It struck me quite suddenly that her drive to split up the Six Pack had been fuelled all along by jealousy. She didn't belong at the riding school, never had. Probably, nobody had ever invited her to join a club before. She'd been on the outside, shunned because of her attitude, an attitude developed from bitterness because she was never really one of the in-crowd.

"Are you planning on letting go of that pole, Stephanie? Or are you going to treat us all to a tango?" Guy was waiting with his arms folded.

I climbed back onto the fence with a warm, leaping sensation coursing through me. Just to be totally sure I pulled out the tickets, feeling the grainy texture of the damp card, and read the official words. Three tickets. It wasn't a hoax. Three of the Six Pack had first row seats at the Josh Le Fleur lecture-demonstration. It was a godsend.

*

"We're going to be late." Sophie sat on the bus, nervously twiddling her hair, as signs for Horseworld flashed past. Jodie was staring out of the window, her chin set in a rigid line which was a tell-tale sign that she was nervous. I'd got to choose who went with me and I'd picked Sophie and Jodie because they were the most mature and sensible. Kate had been put-out because she was the eldest and naturally thought she should be in charge.

I stared out of the window thinking about the legendary Monty Roberts who had started off the phenomenon of talking to horses in their own language. There had been a series of articles in *In the Saddle* about talking to horses. The Six Pack had spent hours in the field trying to achieve the same bond. We'd all been to see *The Horse Whisperer* four times and knew it off by heart. Please, Josh, be able to sort out Monty's problems. If only this total stranger knew he was our very last hope. I spent the rest of the journey pretending to jump telegraph poles in my mind's eye, getting the striding spot on. I'd done this since I was six years old.

"It's packed," said Sophie as we arrived and pushed our way down to the front row, looking for seats twelve, thirteen and fifteen. None of us wanted to sit in seat thirteen but Sophie eventually agreed and plopped herself down saying we were stupidly superstitious.

The indoor school was buzzing with excitement. Slap bang in the centre was a see-through metal pen which was where all the training took place. Somebody was talking on a microphone, going through all Josh le Fleur's achievements. He'd even been working with wild zebra and antelope in Africa. He'd worked on racehorses for royalty and famous showjumpers and once retrained a killer stallion who used to attack anyone who set foot in his stable.

There were lots of oohs and aahs and an electric current of anticipation. The speaker announced there would be refreshments in the break. The most we could run to was a coffee between the three of us.

We weren't prepared for Josh le Fleur. He was about the size of Frankie Dettori with a mop of unruly brown hair and a down-to-earth, almost shy demeanour. It was as if he was embarrassed by his own success.

Two men were leading a huge, heavy Irish Draught horse down the side of the school, keeping a really strong hold on brass chain lead ropes.

"I recognize that horse," said the woman in the next seat, ferreting on the floor excitedly for her programme and turning to the man next to her. "That's O'Riley – belongs to Pip down the road. It chased the vicar out of the field the other day. Nobody can do a thing with it."

101

She leaned forward intently as the men released the horse in the pen and it immediately took a swipe at one of them and thundered round in a rage. Jodie, Sophie and I exchanged startled looks and wondered what would happen next.

Josh stepped inside the pen with nothing but a lunge rein. Everybody in the building fell silent. The horse snorted and stared like a bull. We were convinced it was going to charge him.

And then the magic started. Josh began by quietly driving him away, looking him straight in the eye. O'Riley seemed stunned that someone had the guts to stand up to him and paddled off in the direction Josh wanted. He kept this up for a few minutes and miraculously Josh predicted what he would do next. When O'Riley started lowering his head and making chewing movements with his jaw, that was when Josh dropped his eyes and half turned his back.

The audience gasped as this huge bully of a horse immediately walked after Josh like an innocent baby, zigzagging round the pen after him, his nose touching his shoulder. Everybody clapped like crazy and O'Riley stood stock-still like a transformed horse, enjoying the attention and flapping his rubbery lips as if to say how pleased he was with himself.

After that there followed a procession of different horses. There was a Shetland pony with a terror of horseboxes. A show horse who hated male judges, a racehorse scared of starting stalls and a beautiful Arab who bucked like crazy every time the rider tried to tighten the girth. Josh had them all cured within minutes and could give a detailed account of what had made them so traumatized in the first place. It was as if he could read their minds and talk to them in a way the average person couldn't. He was truly gifted. We were all transfixed. We didn't notice time passing, and had no idea that the bay dressage horse, carefully going through his paces, was the grand finale. And then Josh was summing up, advising owners on how they could get more out of their horses and develop a special bond.

I was in a daze, trying to memorize each word. Suddenly Jodie was leaning close, pointing at her watch. We had to get out of there. Quick.

I leapt up and immediately knocked over a carton of popcorn. Jodie grabbed my coat and we started inching down the aisle, scrabbling over feet and handbags.

"Hurry up," Sophie hissed, bringing up the rear. There was various tutting and some disapproving faces. Josh was still talking. Everyone was now aware of three girls frantically trying to leave the building. I could feel my face flushing brick red. The last man in the row had to stand up to let us pass which took for ever, and in the mean-time Josh was leaving the arena.

"Where now?" I asked frantically. We slid out of the main doors earning an angry look from a woman in a grey suit.

It was dark and cold outside and extremely quiet. We could still hear the microphone: "Unfortunately Mr le Fleur has to leave straight away in order to catch a flight to Los Angeles where he'll be working on a film due out next year. However, there are various books, videos and signed photos on sale, and experienced assistants in the foyer who'll be able to answer any questions." There was a groan of disappointment.

"Come on!" Jodie grabbed my arm. "Run!"

The car park was jam-packed but there was no sign of Josh.

"The back doors," Sophie breathed.

We ran at full pelt down a row of stables, disturbing horses, clattering over a bucket. Sophie streaked ahead – she wasn't a champion cross-country runner at school for nothing. There, by the gate, was a set of headlights, dipped into the hedge.

"It's got to be him!"

We thundered across, my lungs gasping for air, and a stitch searing through my side. The car was black and sleek with someone in the driving seat reading a paper by the interior light. He got out as soon as he saw us. Behind, we heard the click-clack of high heels. It was the woman in the grey suit. And behind her, draped in a cream riding mac, was Josh.

"Mr le Fleur!"

"Oh no, it's those kids again." The woman wrinkled up her face in distaste and hurried her step. "Mr le Fleur is a very busy man. If you'd kindly step aside."

Jodie and Sophie were blocking the car doors – not intentionally, but they didn't move when they realized the delaying tactics of their position.

"Mr le Fleur!" I stepped forward, every nerve in my body zinging with urgency. "Please help us!"

The woman's face set hard. Her voice was raw with irritation. "Would you please step aside."

"It's my pony," I blurted out. "Well, he's a loan pony, but he'll be sent back if ... Please, Mr le Fleur, he's terrified of traffic. We've only got until tomorrow." I babbled on, frantic, desperate.

"I'm sorry, but I've got a plane to catch." He said it firmly, trying to smile.

"You're our last chance," I pleaded, pushing my hair back behind my ears, wishing I wasn't so young, so insignificant. "You said you wanted to help horses and ponies all over the world, and not just the expensive ones."

He paused, faltering for the first time in his hurry to get to the car.

"Please, Mr le Fleur. Monty needs help. He's screwed up. I don't know what to do to help him." I felt my voice start to shake. My eyes filled with tears and I brushed them away impatiently.

"Monty, you say . . ." He was thinking, considering.

"We really must get a move on," said the woman, fidgeting, panicking, trying to urge him on.

Seizing the moment I spilled out the story of Georgie Fenton, the accident, the Six Pack, Abby and the test tomorrow.

"You're our last chance," I pleaded. "I know you can cure him." At that moment I would have gladly gone down on my knees and begged.

"How far away is this riding school did you say?"

Relief washed over me in great waves.

"We really need to be at the airport . . ."

"Later," Josh waved his hand dismissively, his eyes bright with sudden excitement and urgency. "I think you and your friends had better get in the car, don't you?"

Chapter Ten

"My brain feels like scrambled eggs." Abby shot up in bed, clearly remembering what day it was.

I dragged myself out of sleep, suddenly feeling sick with nerves. Abby's test was at 2.30 p.m. Then we'd know for definite whether the training had worked.

"Happy Birthday," said Abby, looking pale as she headed for the bathroom.

I glanced at the lovely glossy photograph of Monty on my dressing table and counted off twelve years on my fingers. "Happy Birthday – *not*," I mumbled, feeling my stomach flip over.

Josh's visit to Brook House had been incredible. Everybody knew who he was and I couldn't believe we'd got his sole attention. He treated Monty as if he were a racehorse belonging to the queen. Other girls in riding hats and jods hung around, hoping to get a look in, but Josh got straight on with the job in hand, totally focused on Monty's condition.

To start with he worked at gaining his trust,

without even going near a car. Very soon Monty was following him around like a devoted puppy. He looked like the old Monty, his brown eyes relaxed and fearless.

Sophie clutched my elbow. She was as excited as I felt. Abby was screwing up her face, watching the whole procedure in awe. This was Monty's chance to be normal again.

When Josh finally asked the woman in the grey suit to switch the engine on in his car we were all so nervous we could hardly breathe. Rachel and Emma were so obviously star-struck, they hadn't said a word since Josh had arrived.

"I wish he could do this to humans," Kate whispered. "I'd ask him to stop me from being scared of jumps, and to be able to pass exams without throwing up."

"He's a top class horse trainer," Jodie hissed, ultra-serious, "Not a genie in a lamp."

"All right, don't get uptight. I was only saying."

"Well don't."

Monty was approaching the car. At first he seemed tense. He snorted once. Josh circled round him, not looking him in the eye, and then walked closer, waiting for him to follow. There was no pressure on the lead rope. Monty shrugged, almost as a human would, and clamped onto Josh's shoulder, as close to him as was physically possible.

"Come on, Monty," I whispered, crossing my fingers.

Monty tentatively stepped closer, his forelegs shaking as he lifted each one from the ground. The soft purr of the engine seemed to roar in my ears, louder and louder. Monty was right next to the car and he still hadn't pulled back.

Amazingly, Josh opened the bonnet so Monty could see the engine whirring, hear the noise more loudly, smell the oil. Still he didn't pull back, but just pushed his nose into the crook of Josh's arm, seeking safety.

Josh asked for a bucket of feed which Sophie ran off to fetch. I desperately wanted to go up to Monty but knew I'd break the magic spell. Monty was totally focused on Josh. If a jumbo jet had landed I still don't think he'd have flinched.

Sophie quietly passed the feed bucket to Josh who placed it on the bonnet of the car. Miraculously, with a little encouragement Monty started eating from the bucket, his chest only inches from the sleek bonnet. All the time, Josh talked to him, ran his hands all over his body, under his stomach, his back, down each leg. We could all see Monty relaxing. All the tension of the last week draining out. In fact, by the time he'd finished the horse nuts, he looked half asleep.

Josh then got his assistant to drive the car back and forth past Monty, revving the engine as loud as she could. The whole Six Pack braced themseles anxiously. Even Rocket, or Buzby or Rusty wouldn't tolerate that. In fact no horse or pony at the riding school would. Monty blinked curiously and then even rested a hind leg! It was a miracle! He was cured!

Josh finally let us go up to him and pat him and hug him. Then Sophie, being the most socially confident of all of us, hugged Josh, and Kate asked for his autograph which he scribbled on a match-box. I buried my hands into Monty's thick mane and didn't know whether to laugh or cry.

"Now I really do have a plane to catch," said Josh glancing anxiously at his watch.

"How can we ever thank you?" I felt dizzy with emotion.

"No, thank *you*," he replied, rubbing Monty's nose one more time, "for asking me to help. For going to such lengths."

The car pulled away, turned right and quickly disappeared. All we had to worry about now was the test. And whether Monty would remember what he'd just been taught. Or anything at all.

Margaret had cooked a full English breakfast with mushroom, sausage and the crispiest of bacon. Beside my place was a birthday card and a tiny present which, when I opened it, held two tiny gold earrings in the shape of horseshoes. Just what I wanted. Inside the birthday card was a simple message – Good Luck for today.

I carefully stood it up next to the ones from Dad and Mum and glanced across to the door handle where my black show jacket was hanging, brushed and cleaned to perfection.

"Thanks," I said and meant it. "For everything."

Then I picked up my knife and fork and tackled the huge breakfast. I cleaned my plate for the first time since Margaret had married Dad and she flushed with pleasure. Everything wasn't totally OK yet but at least we were all heading in the right direction. We wanted to be a family and that's what mattered most.

We were determined to give Abby one last chance to get the hang of rising trot. As soon as we arrived at the riding school we tacked up and headed for the field. We were going to position ourselves as before, but this time Sophie was going to ride Rocket alongside in the hope that Abby might fall in with her rhythm.

It was a clear, fresh morning and Monty shone like the sunshine itself. Abby tightened her reins and, lost in concentration, drew level with Rocket. Kate clipped a lead rope on Monty's bit and led him forward.

"Up, down, up, down, up, down. Come on, Abby, up, down. One, two, one, two." She was bumping valiantly, her face grim with determination. Rachel took over, chanting the rhythm. Abby fixed her eyes on Sophie, watching her rise up and down on Rocket. She looked as if she was about to burst with frustration.

"Come on, Abby!"

Jane and Serena happened to be riding down the drive, legs loose, out of the stirrups, shoulders slack, slouched in the saddle. They started tittering and I knew why. Rage ripped through me and I fixed my eyes on Abby bouncing towards me.

"*Abby. Up. Now!*"

Her head darted up, her riding hat slipped down and she levered her seat up just at the right moment. One. Two. One, two, one two. She'd got it. She was doing rising trot. Her face lit up incredulously and Kate yelled out in sheer disbelief, "She's got it, Abby's doing rising trot!"

After that it was easy. She walked, trotted and cantered round the field by herself, in perfect balance. Monty didn't put a foot wrong. I'd never seen anybody so ecstatic. She showered him with pats and kisses and slithered to the ground with dimples showing in her cheeks from grinning so much.

"Wait till I tell my mates back home about this. I can ride, really truly ride, and not a plod either – a proper horse." I didn't pull her up about Monty being a pony, not a horse because I was too taken

112

aback. It was the first time she'd ever mentioned her life "back home".

An outline of the road safety course was pinned up on the saloon noticeboard. It was marked in a red pen. Red for danger. Abby suddenly seemed to have turned a very funny colour.

I was to take my test on Blossom, a cute little Welsh Mountain who could be awkward if you didn't show her who was boss from the very beginning. Emma groaned when she saw we had to ride down a stretch of road with luscious grass verges on each side.

"Buzby will stick his head down for sure. I'd better superglue my hands to the reins."

"That pony needs his jaw wiring up," Kate said matter-of-factly, somehow finding the appetite to eat a cream bun.

"By the looks of it, so do you."

The test was divided into two parts, one on the actual roads, and another in the back field, which was a mock test with lots of hazards – pretend roadworks, traffic lights and noisy pedestrians. There was even a mock road junction where we had to use arm signals.

"What do they think we're riding? Police horses?" Jodie was looking increasingly alarmed, mainly because she was riding Minstrel, an Arab who spooked if a crisp bag blew past. She didn't know how he'd react when confronted with people having picnics and road closed signs and tractors and trailers.

Abby's eyes locked onto the tractor which was the last hazard on the test. Stewards would be standing at various points to mark down a pass or fail.

"I think I'm just going to go for a little walk," Abby whispered suddenly, and wandered off looking distinctly shaky.

"It's for you." Guy left the brown parcel on the saloon table, swivelling it round so I could read the label. To the Six Pack. From Josh le Fleur. "Someone dropped it off five minutes ago – said it was urgent."

We gazed at the wrapping for ages and then Kate took the initiative, ripped off the string and pulled at one corner. Inside was a simple black box with a clasp. Kate prised it open and gasped in delight. On a velvet background, all in a line, were oval badges, navy blue and gold rimmed with a tiny riding hat and crop in the centre. They were beautiful.

"Here's a note." Sophie unfolded a piece of paper.

Dear girls,
    Every exclusive club needs a membership

badge. Hope these will suffice. Keep up your
special work.

From one of your supporters, Josh.

It was amazing. Nobody had ever taken us this
seriously before. In absolute reverence, Sophie
carefully pinned the badges onto our riding shirts
until there was just one left.

"I'd better find Abby," I said picking up the
other badge and slipping it into my pocket. Thankfully Josh had thought of everybody.

"Number sixteen, number sixteen, kindly ride
forward." The pony club District Commissioner
had commandeered the loudspeaker and was
frightening the ponies even more than the so-called
hazards. The Sutton Vale members were having
terrible problems keeping their ponies under
control. They looked suspiciously like they had
been fed oats. One tank-like pony had careered
straight through the picnic hazard and was
charging around with a tablecloth hanging from
his stirrups.

Guy was trying to organize twelve riding school
ponies to appear on time and looking presentable
with the appropriate rider on board. Two whining
girls in over-large back protectors were com-
plaining that they'd put their names down to ride
Rusty.

Rusty had just done a perfect test with Rachel, not batting an eyelid and earning top marks. Rachel was thrilled and started advising Kate who was panicking big time because Archie wouldn't move past the portable loo.

I'd left Monty in the stable, right till the last possible moment. Anything to keep him as calm as possible. Blossom stood idly switching flies and blowing herself up so that I couldn't tighten her girth. Abby was nervously chewing her nails, waiting for me to finish so she could change into my riding clothes.

"Oh no!" Sophie groaned out loud. Minstrel had just had a bucking fit and thrown Jodie into the pretend zebra crossing. "This is unbearable." She could hardly stand the tension any longer.

I felt as if the ground was rearing up at me, my throat suddenly desert-dry and throbbing. I'd just spotted Dad and Margaret walking casually towards the marked out course. And not alone. I'd recognize the short, blond couple anywhere – they were Monty's loan owners. They could only be here for one reason – to take him back. How could Dad do this to me? And on my birthday of all days. Hot, stinging tears built up at the back of my eyes.

I'd rarely seen Sophie so stirred up. "Dad, this is so unfair," she said, tripping after Mr Green who was stalking around, spreading gloom everywhere.

Rachel and Abby were leading Monty up from the stables. He was quietly observing all the activity, perfectly relaxed, walking like a famous racehorse, his mane and tail plaited, his hoofs oiled. He looked stunning.

"Dad, you can't go through with this. It's ridiculous."

Mr Green swung round and glared fiercely at his daughter, but we all knew it was a front – he adored her really, just wanted the best for her. That had always been the trouble. "Sophie, don't try and undermine my authority. I've made my decision and I'm not backing down. No, Sophie." She opened her mouth to answer back. "Just drop it. Please."

Abby sat on Monty, ramrod straight, her elbows carefully in at her sides. Only her nervous smile indicated that she was anything but calm.

"You can only do your best," I reassured her, reaching up and gripping her wrist. "You've already done your best. You've moved mountains to get this far. If he plays up you've got to get straight off. Don't even try to ride him." My voice tailed off. There was nothing left to say. Abby gave me a quick, bright little smile and pulled herself up to her full height in the saddle.

She was to do the road safety test first and as she came into the back field to tackle the hazards she was to stick up her thumb if everything had gone well.

Monty stood like an angel. I wrapped my arms round his solid neck, trying to breathe confidence into him. Dear, darling Monty. It was so important that Josh's training had worked. If it hadn't . . . I couldn't even bear to contemplate it. I turned away, tears pressing at the back of my eyes. Abby rode forward towards the first steward.

"Steph!" Dad's voice burst into my thoughts. He was coming towards me, waving, Margaret and the other couple tagging along, trying to keep up.

"Quick, hide me." I dived behind Emma and Kate who shuffled forward, shielding me from view. I couldn't talk to Dad now. In fact, after Monty went, I didn't think I'd ever be able to talk to him again.

"She's here!" Sophie was the first to spot Monty and Abby coming back into the field. Monty was walking with even steps, his nose tucked in, Abby was staring straight ahead, her jaw jutting out.

"Over here!" Sophie called. A cold tentacle of fear crept up my neck. Why hadn't she seen us? Then she stuck up her thumb. She was grinning.

"She's passed," Emma leapt in the air, swinging an arm round my neck.

"Has she? Really?" I could feel my face burning, my heart thudding. She was trotting now and two stewards were calling her number. This was the

118

final hurdle – the pretend zebra crossing, the road-works, the tractor.

Monty stepped forward timidly.

"She needs to use more leg." Sophie stuck her knuckle in her mouth and started biting it.

Emma was standing on my foot but I didn't really notice. No amount of physical pain could compare to what was going on inside me.

"My nerves are in shreds," moaned Emma, screwing her eyes shut as Monty approached the roadworks.

"He's through." Rachel was the only one who could watch calmly.

"Steady! Careful!" Abby was trotting, rising too high, too fast . . .

"She's past the picnic site." For one awful moment Abby lost her balance and nearly fell off.

The tractor roared into life.

"Now we'll know," said Sophie, linking arms with me and Jodie. "He'll do it. I know he will. He's got to."

Over by the start rope Mr Green watched care-fully. Monty pricked up his ears, alert. I saw Abby patting his shoulder and talking to him with words of encouragement. I felt a stab of panic as he halted suddenly then moved forward. I could hardly bear it.

Abby sat up straight and shortened her reins. It was all down to Josh's training now. Monty thought for a moment, then miraculously he walked confidently past. He was the best pony in the world – a legend!

Abby let out a whoop of delight and rode back to the Six Pack who were clapping and cheering. It was brilliant. Monty was road-safe with a certificate to prove it.

"Stephanie!" Suddenly there was Dad pushing his way through. Happiness drained away. Monty was going back to his loan owners. They probably had the horsebox parked outside now. I managed a watery smile, all anger and resentment gone – I was just too exhausted.

"We've bought Monty!" he yelled, rushing up to me. "That's what you wanted, isn't it? For your birthday?"

The rest of the day was sheer bliss. I had loads of lovely presents from my friends and we ended up having a proper picnic with all the ponies gathered round munching on carrot sandwiches made by Kate. Monty knew he was the star attraction and kept pawing the ground, knocking over plastic cups of stewed tea. Buzby ate his road safety rosette which caused a huge laugh.

I couldn't stop looking at Monty's gorgeous, alert head. He was mine to keep, groom, ride, look after for ever.

Later on, when we were about to go home, I tracked down Abby for a very formal announcement. We wanted her to join the Six Pack as an official member.

"I'd best not." Abbey smiled nervously, unsure.

I was really taken aback.

"You see, I'm going back to live with Dad, just as soon as mum sorts my stuff out."

The breath practically left my body. "I know I've been awful, really mean, but it's not like that any more. I love having you around – I've always wanted a sister."

Abby smiled, almost mischievous. "It's not that. I'm just missing my own mates, my own bedroom. I'll come back in the holidays. And you'd better send photos and write lots. I want to know all about Monty." She looked across to where he was staring out over the field gate, relaxed and happy. "Anyway," she said, nudging my arm, "I'm going to check out my local riding school, maybe form a Six Pack all of my own. What do you say?"

"I think that's an excellent idea." I knew that Abby wasn't just talking. She was the most determined person ever. "One thing's for sure," I said, thinking about all the horses and ponies and my friends at Brook House, "riding school life is just the best in the world."

A selected list of SAMANTHA ALEXANDER books available from Macmillan

The prices shown below are correct at the time of going to press. However, Macmillan Publishers reserve the right to show new retail prices on covers which may differ from those previously advertised.

RIDING SCHOOL

1. Jodie	0 330 36836 2	£2.99
2. Emma	0 330 36837 0	£2.99
3. Steph	0 330 36838 9	£2.99
4. Kate	0 330 36839 7	£2.99
5. Sophie	0 330 36840 0	£2.99
6. Rachel	0 330 36841 9	£2.99

HOLLYWELL STABLES

1. Flying Start	0 330 33639 8	£2.99
2. The Gamble	0 330 33685 1	£2.99
3. The Chase	0 330 33857 9	£2.99
4. Fame	0 330 33858 7	£2.99

All Macmillan titles can be ordered at your local bookshop or are available by post from:

Book Service by Post
PO Box 29, Douglas, Isle of Man IM99 1BQ

Credit cards accepted. For details:
Telephone: 01624 675137
Fax: 01624 670923
E-mail: bookshop@enterprise.net

Free postage and packing in the UK.
Overseas customers: add £1 per book (paperback)
and £3 per book (hardback).